CHILLS

SECOND STAR
to the FRIGHT

Disney CHILLS

SECOND STAR
to the FRIGHT

by

Vera Strange

Disney PRESS

Los Angeles · New York

The dreams that you FEAR will come true.

1
THE BIG FRIGHT

"**R**ise and shine!"

Barrie's mother's voice echoed through the house, up the stairs, down the hallway, and through his bedroom door. "Time to get up for school."

How does she have vocal superpowers that could wake the dead? Barrie thought as he buried his head under his pillow. He cracked his eyes open and groaned when he saw the clock.

"Not even *six*," he muttered into his pillow, pressing his head into it. He grasped at the last fleeting tendrils of sleep and the exciting dream he'd been having, not wanting to forget it. He'd been trying to solve a mystery in a haunted cabin on a remote island, looking for a secret treasure. "It's still dark outside. This is . . . *child torture*."

He flipped over and tried to bury his head deeper, knocking the pile of mystery books off his bed and onto the floor, along with the flashlight that he'd used to stay up late reading well past his bedtime. His eyes darted to one of the books on the floor. The cover read *The Mystery of Cabin Island*. Clearly, the dream was inspired by his late-night reading. He could tell the exact spot where he'd left off and fallen asleep from the deep crease in the spine.

Barrie loved reading mystery books more than anything. He loved the way they made his heart thump in excitement as he read faster and faster, his fingers flipping the pages to get to the end and discover how the characters solved the case. In real life, he often found himself sneaking off to look for secret treasures and slipping down dark hallways and into places he didn't belong. He wished his real life was as exciting as that of the band of sleuthing brothers from his books.

Before he could remember if he'd solved the mystery and found the hidden treasure in his dream, the door to his bedroom burst open and startled him, making the whole thing evaporate from his mind.

Bright, artificial light spilled in from the hallway, making his eyes tear up. He ducked under the pillow once more.

"Is my little guy ready for a brand-new day?" Mom called in a singsong voice. "The early bird gets the worm!"

Getting a worm? That's how she was trying to motivate him to wake up?

Barrie couldn't understand how anyone could be this cheerful so early, let alone on a school day. It was one of life's greatest mysteries, even more than the ones in his books.

"I'm up . . . I'm up . . . I swear," Barrie muttered. He tried to sound convincing.

But even he knew he'd failed.

"Don't make me come back up here," she warned, shifting into her stern mom voice like she'd flipped a light switch. It was another one of her superpowers. "You're almost twelve now," she went on. "You know what that means."

"Uh, what?" Barrie said, his voice muffled by the pillow that was keeping the light from searing his eyeballs. He lifted his head and tried to pry them open again. His mom looked blurry.

"Old enough to get yourself up for school," she finished. Her gaze darted to the pile of books and the flashlight on the floor. *Busted*. "We'll discuss that later. Now get up!"

Before he could respond, Barrie heard her footsteps retreating across the carpeted hall, then her rapping on his sister's door.

"Rita, that means you, too," Mom continued. "You're even worse than your little brother."

Oh, good. If she was going after Rita, that would buy him a little time. He tried to snooze a bit more, but he could hear her raised voice reverberating through the house.

Ever since Mom got downsized from her job as a copy editor at a magazine last month and started freelancing from home, she'd been more stressed than usual. Dad had picked up more shifts at the power plant where he worked as a civil engineer, but it didn't make up for the lost income—or so Barrie had overheard when he'd been practicing his sleuthing skills. Apparently, freelance magazine work was scarce right now, and even Barrie could see the bills were piling up on the kitchen table. Just last night, his parents had been arguing about it, and he hadn't even had to snoop to hear that conversation. He'd been reading in bed when he was supposed to be sleeping, and they'd gotten loud enough for him to take in every word.

"You just had your sixteenth birthday," Mom yelled at Rita, her raised voice forcing him to finally, truly wake. "You can pitch in and help out more. Oh, and don't forget. Starting today, you get to drive your brother's school carpool."

"Ugh, don't remind me," Rita complained. "Him and his goober friends are gonna smear hazardous waste all over my back seat."

"That was our deal, remember?" Mom said. "I took you to get your license. You can drive the carpool."

"Fine, but I need the bleach wipes," Rita griped. "Like a whole canister to decontaminate my car."

"Please, don't be so melodramatic," Mom said with an

exasperated sigh. "I've been driving you both around for years. How do you think I feel?"

"Have you seen the bathroom after he showers?" Rita said. "And what's that smell that leaches out of his closet?"

"Fine, you make a good point," Mom said finally. "I'll leave the wipes out in the kitchen. Which reminds me . . . a new list of chores is waiting for you down there— including cleaning the bathroom."

"Anything *but* the bathroom," Rita said. "Please have mercy on my soul!"

Barrie forced himself out of bed. It wasn't like he was going to get back to sleep now with Rita moaning and wailing at the top of her lungs. If he'd learned anything about what happened when you became a teenager, it was that everything turned into a huge drama.

A few weeks earlier, Rita had been gifted a blowout sweet sixteen party, complete with a DJ and dance floor. But ever since her birthday, all his parents could talk about was how she needed to "grow up" and "pitch in more around the house."

Being almost twelve was bad enough, but turning

sixteen looked even worse. What happened when you became an actual adult?

Growing up is the worst, Barrie decided, pulling on jeans and a sweatshirt. He missed being a little kid, when he could watch cartoons and play all day and didn't have to get up early for school.

He patted down his curly hair, trying to tame it into submission, and caught sight of his reflection in the mirror. He had chubby cheeks, still full of baby fat and dotted with freckles. His eyes were hazel, a mixture of brown and green; that he liked. But basically, he looked like any ordinary twelve-year-old.

Well, *almost* twelve-year-old.

"I wish I could stay a kid forever," he whispered to his reflection.

As he got dressed, he caught a whiff of his closet and scrunched up his nose. Okay, maybe his sister did have a point about the smell. Of course, his mom had told him like a *bazillion* times to clean it out, but he always seemed to have better things to do, like play video games or skateboard in the park with his friends or read his pile of mystery books.

He could worry about having a clean closet when he got older, couldn't he?

Barrie slammed the closet door and grabbed his backpack, then bounded downstairs to the kitchen. He was still half asleep, but luckily, he could navigate his house on autopilot. They'd lived there since he was born.

Before he could pour himself cereal or sit down at the table, Dad caught his eye. That pile of bills sat next to him and somehow looked even taller than it had last night.

"Did you finish your homework?" his father asked.

Another terrible thing about growing up. *Homework.* Every year, it got harder and took longer, too. He was one week away from graduating from elementary school and moving up to sixth grade. The graduation ceremony was next Friday. He'd be attending New London Junior High School in the fall. But first, he'd have a glorious three months of summer break, where he didn't have to worry about anything other than being a kid and having fun.

"Uh, yeah mostly," Barrie said, fudging. The truth was . . . he hadn't done any of it. He'd just gotten so caught up in his new book. He'd have to try to copy off Michael and John, his best friends. He just hoped they had actually done the homework and not goofed off like him.

"Well, if we find out you didn't," Mom chimed in cheerfully, "you'll get grounded again." She took a sip from her giant cup of coffee.

Barrie eyed his parents over the breakfast table. They both looked . . . *tired*.

Despite them insisting that waking up early was a good thing, they both had dark circles under their eyes and chugged coffee like their lives depended on it. Even now, his mom was downing her fresh cup in a few swallows. Her coffee intake had definitely risen since the layoff and transition to working from home, and the living room had become her de facto office. It was covered in random pieces of paper and draped with power cords for various electronic devices. Everything had changed, and not for the better.

"Just wait for high school," Rita said in a snarky voice, pouring a bowl of healthy cereal and adding almond milk. "It gets a lot harder. You'll have even more homework—plus *algebra*."

The way his sister pronounced *algebra* made it sound

like a curse word. His eyes darted to her backpack, slumped by the front door. It was overflowing with thick textbooks.

"Uh, I'm not even sure what that is," Barrie said, bypassing the healthy options and pouring himself a bowl of his favorite sugary cereal with a friendly-looking cartoon pirate gracing the box. "Fractions are bad enough."

"It's like fractions *times* a million," Rita said, aiming her milk-encrusted spoon at his face. "Trust me, you'll hate it—"

"Rita, don't scare your little brother like that." Dad cut her off, slurping coffee. "Algebra is great fun."

Rita looked horrified. "Uh, how is algebra *fun*? Are you losing it? Nobody likes algebra. It's like a scientific fact. They've proven it in actual studies."

"Right . . . let's see . . . things we couldn't do without algebra . . ." Dad mused. "It's how we got to the moon."

Barrie shot his father a skeptical look. He knew for a fact that parents lied to kids a lot. Like *white* lies. *Little* lies. It was almost like they didn't want kids to realize the truth about what it was really like to grow up.

"The moon?" Rita said with a snort. "Uh, that's the best you've got? Can *algebra* get me out of car-pool, too?"

"Rita, we discussed this already," Mom called from across the kitchen, shooting her a chastising look. "We had an agreement, remember?"

But then she brightened and tapped the family wall calendar. "Excited for your birthday next week, Little Guy?"

She pointed to the square for Monday. On it was a crude drawing of balloons and a birthday cake, along with the scrawled words:

BARRIE'S 12th birthday

The week was packed with other appointments, including his graduation ceremony on Friday, which promised to be excruciatingly boring and feature a cameo by his annoying aunt Wanda and twin cousins, who were both drooling, snotty toddlers.

But then there was also the one thing that he'd been looking forward to for months. His eyes locked on the square for Tuesday, and he felt a rush of excitement jolt through him.

"Yeah, how would you like to celebrate?" Dad chimed in. "I mean, besides going to the Lost Boys concert with your friends on Tuesday night and rocking out."

Barrie cringed when his dad said *rocking out*. Somehow it sounded cool when his friends said that kind of stuff. But not when his father tried it.

The Lost Boys were their favorite band. His parents had gotten him a ticket as a gift for his birthday and agreed to extend his curfew since he was turning twelve and graduating from elementary school. Michael and John had also convinced their parents and scored tickets to the sold-out concert. They were all going together. It was like some kind of sign—his favorite band coming to town the day after his birthday. Barrie couldn't wait.

"Let's see . . . oh, I know!" Dad went on, tapping at his tablet with great enthusiasm. "What about a family trip to the maritime museum this weekend?"

His father smiled at him expectantly. Barrie frowned, fiddling with his spoon. While not as bad as algebra, that didn't sound like much fun.

"Uh, what's a . . . maritime museum?" he asked cautiously.

"Oh, it's super exciting!" Dad said in a voice that made Barrie pretty sure that it was the exact opposite.

His father pulled up the website on his tablet, then flipped it around for Barrie to see. Images of old ships flashed across the screen, under the heading "The New London Maritime Museum—Where History Comes To Life!"

"It's located out by the marina," Dad said, tapping again at the screen. "It's a museum dedicated to naval history."

"What's that mean?" Barrie said.

"It means *boats*, Goober," Rita said snarkily. She loved showing off how much more she knew than he did.

"And not just *any* boats," Dad added, flipping through the website. "This museum specializes in pirate history."

He pointed to a ship with a black-and-white flag printed with a skull and crossbones. The name was painted across the hull in ornate script:

Jolly Roger

Barrie studied the image, feeling unsettled. The skull seemed to stare into his soul.

"You can even tour an old pirate ship," Dad went on. "Doesn't that sound amazing?"

"Uh . . . maybe," Barrie hedged, not wanting to disappoint his dad. But what he really wanted to do was to hit the skate park with his friends, not tour some boring old boat museum.

His father was a big history buff. He loved anything tied to the past. But most of that stuff was just boring if you asked Barrie — or saw his straight B minuses on his history quizzes. It all happened a long time ago, so why should he care?

"Great, then I'll grab tickets," Dad went on, oblivious to his son's total lack of interest. "The whole family can go on Sunday. We can have some nice family time."

Now it was Rita's turn to look stricken. "But I was supposed to see a movie with my friends—"

"Rita, it's for your brother's birthday," Mom said in her stern voice. "You can see a movie with your friends another time."

"Yeah, stop behaving like a kid and act your age," Dad added with a frown.

Rita flung her spoon down and pouted, but she knew better than to argue the point further. That could only result in the worst-case scenario for any teen — losing car or phone privileges. Or worse yet, getting grounded.

Mom ignored Rita's silent temper tantrum, which happened on a regular basis, and turned her attention to Barrie.

"Then, on Monday, you can have a party at the skate park with your friends after school," she said. "On your actual birthday. How does that sound?"

"Oh, I can?" Barrie said, perking up and feeling slightly better. "And I can still go to the concert on Tuesday, too?"

"Yup, it's not every day my little guy turns *twelve*. How about a cake?" Mom said, picking up her phone to call in the order. "What flavor?"

"Triple chocolate fudge!" the whole family said in unison, then laughed. It had been Barrie's favorite since before he could talk.

"Good choice, Son," Dad added, still chuckling.

Even Rita couldn't think of anything snarky or negative to say about *chocolate*.

"Love you," Barrie said with a grin. His parents really were the best, even if they annoyed him sometimes.

He finished his cereal; then Mom informed them that they were going to be late for school. Still in a bad mood—though lately, that seemed to be her natural state—Rita grabbed her keys, backpack, and the canister of bleach wipes.

"Come on, Goober," she said in a pouty voice. "Let's get this over with."

Barrie picked up his backpack and followed her toward the front door. He turned back to say goodbye to his parents. His father was still studying the maritime museum website.

Suddenly, an image of a pirate flashed onto the screen—beady eyes, long black hair, and a thin black mustache. He sported a crimson jacket and large pirate hat with a fluffy feather sprouting out of the ornate ribbon.

But that wasn't what caught Barrie's attention. Instead of a hand, his left arm ended in a silver hook. Barrie's eyes darted to the bold headline at the top of the website: The Mystery of Captain Hook and His Missing Hand.

It reminded Barrie of the mysteries in his books. Only, this was a real-life mystery.

But before he could really consider it, Rita grabbed him by the backpack, dragging him through the front door.

"Don't you dare touch anything in my car," she hissed under her breath. "Or, I'll make you walk the plank."

"Aye, aye, matey," Barrie said, promising himself that he'd smear boogers on the door handle just to teach her a lesson. She obviously deserved it.

2

BLASTED CARPOOL

"**L**emme see your hands, Goobers," Rita said, passing out sanitizer wipes to Barrie, Michael, and John. She narrowed her eyes. "Drop the cheese puffs, Michael."

She was supposed to be picking them up after school, but she stood blocking the door to her sky-blue electric car. Their parents had bought it used for her sixteenth birthday with the promise that she'd take over driving the school carpool. The car was her most prized possession— the ticket to her freedom and nights out with her friends.

And lately, Barrie had noticed that impressing her friends was all Rita seemed to care about. She spent hours primping in the bathroom, curling her hair, and applying endless layers of makeup. If she wasn't doing that, she was texting them on her phone and trying to make them laugh. She constantly worried about what they thought—yet another reason being a teenager seemed like no fun.

Barrie loved his two best friends. He didn't have to worry about impressing them, or what outfit he wore to school, or if his naturally curly hair was frizzing out. They'd known each other since they'd been assigned to the same table in kindergarten, and he knew that they'd be best friends forever. They called themselves the Lost Boys, after their favorite band, of course. They even had a secret handshake and a special knock that they used to sneak through each other's windows after curfew so they could play video games. Their families even lived on the same cul-de-sac, which made the covert activity that much easier.

Michael, who was the shorter and stockier of Barrie's two friends, clutched the bag of cheese puffs protectively, but Rita yanked them out of his florescent-orange fingers.

"Hey, I was still eating those!" Michael yelped. She ignored him and tossed the bag in the trash.

"My carpool, my rules," Rita said, leveling them each

with a penetrating stare. "I know that Mom was lax and let you do whatever the heck you wanted to her car, but there's a new captain in town. You do what I say—or else."

"Dude, your sister is mucho scary," John whispered to Barrie and Michael, as he wiped his long fingers with one of her wipes. John was tall and reed-thin. He and Michael used to joke that when they stood next to each other, they resembled the number ten.

"Seriously," Michael said, glancing mournfully at his discarded cheese puff bag.

Each of them dutifully finished wiping their hands under Rita's close watch, then piled into her back seat. Barrie didn't dare try to ride shotgun. The last thing his sister wanted was to be seen sitting with her little brother. Plus, he wanted to sit next to his friends.

They pulled away from the school. Barrie watched the building fade away in the rearview mirror. He'd had a terrible day that started with him getting busted by Mr. Bates for not completing his math homework, so he had to stay inside during recess to catch up, and it ended with even *more* math homework getting piled on top of his desk.

It was his birthday weekend. The last thing he wanted to do was homework.

And he knew it would only get worse as he got older. Next Friday, he'd graduate and officially be in junior high. His eyes fell on Rita's overflowing backpack in the front passenger seat.

It could be worse, he thought. *I could be in high school.*

Rita followed the familiar route home through their quaint town of New London. The road snaked past the ocean, where steep cliffs plunged down to the rocky beach. Waves lapped up at the rocks, eroding them slowly.

In the distance, Barrie could just make out the marina by the masts of the many ships and boats docked there. Clouds hung in the sky, occasionally spattering the windows with raindrops.

As the car came to a stop at a red light, Barrie reached for the window button, but Rita clicked the child safety lock before he could hit it.

"What did I say, Goober?" she said, catching his eye. "Repeat it back to me."

"Uh, your carpool . . . your rules?" Barrie stammered back.

"Yup, that's right. Don't touch anything back there," Rita said, turning around to glare at them. "Or you will each die horrible, painful, excruciating deaths. Got it?"

"Dude, your sister's not kidding. She might actually kill us," John whispered. "She should keep her eyes on the road at all times. Hands at ten and two. That's a thing, right?"

"Hey, what if she tries to text while driving?" Michael whispered, nervously eying her phone in the center console. "Do we call the cops on her?"

"Trust me, she does not want to get grounded and lose her car privileges," Barrie whispered. "All she cares about is hanging out with her cool friends."

The light turned green, and Rita had no choice but to focus on the road. Barrie relaxed slightly. At least carpool with his sister was less boring than carpool with his mom. And Rita was a decent driver . . . not that he was surprised. His sister was usually pretty responsible.

Well . . . for a teenager, to quote his parents.

Rita switched on the radio. A familiar song blared out of the speakers. It was the Lost Boys' new hit single, "Never Land."

"Your birthday is almost here," Michael said to Barrie, punching his arm playfully. "Lost Boys concert, here we come!" He broke into an air guitar jam as the song hit the upbeat pop chorus.

"*Second star to the right and straight on till morning,*" the three of them sang along. Even Rita bopped her head along to the catchy tune. Nobody could resist it.

"Yeah, can't wait. It's gonna rock," Barrie said with a grin. "But first, I have to go to the maritime museum with my family this weekend." He rolled his eyes at the thought.

"The maritime museum?" John said. "What's that?"

"Uh, like some kind of stupid boat museum," Barrie said. "We're going on Sunday. My dad loves that history stuff. But it looks pretty boring if you ask me."

"Nah, it's dope," Michael said, perking up. "My family went last year when my cousins visited from Maine. The pirate stuff is the best part!"

"Oh, right," Barrie said, remembering the picture on the website that morning. "Wasn't there, like, some famous pirate captain?"

"Yup," Michael said. "Apparently, he was the most

dangerous and bloodthirsty pirate on the high seas! There are all kinds of sick stories about his misadventures."

"Like what?" Barrie asked.

"Well, I don't remember," Michael admitted. "I wasn't paying that much attention on the tour. But there's a real pirate ship you get to go inside. And instead of a hand, he has a hook."

"A hook?" John said nervously.

"I know! I saw the picture," Barrie said. "Do they really not know how he lost his hand?"

"Nope. Nobody knows," Michael said. "It's like some kind of mega mystery. Even the tour guide didn't know."

"A real-life mystery," Barrie said quietly, intrigued. He'd always wanted to solve a real-life mystery, like the boys in his books. "I wonder what happened to it. Do you think someone chopped it off with a sword? Or maybe it got caught up in the ropes on the ship during a storm and just, like, popped off."

"Ew!" John cried.

"And why does he wear a hook?" Barrie wondered.

"Argh, matey!" Michael growled, slashing at them both with his index finger curled into a hook.

Barrie and John both flinched back, but then they all burst out laughing.

"Lost Boys forever," Michael said, reaching out his hand.

They executed their secret group handshake, gripping each other's wrists, then sliding their hands apart and shimmying their shoulders.

"Never grow up," John added.

"*Never*," Barrie agreed. "Kids forever." But the second the words left his lips, he felt a thump of foreboding. "Look . . . I know we're graduating on Friday. But we're gonna stay friends, right? Even in junior high?"

"Like major duh," Michael said. "Changing schools won't change us."

"Yeah, and we're gonna have a blast this summer," John added.

They all grinned at each other. Barrie felt relieved. The stress of that morning and his terrible day at school began to melt away. He had the best friends in the whole entire world.

Just then, they stopped at another stoplight, and a cherry-red convertible pulled up next to them.

Rita turned around in a panic. "Hide, you goobers! I mean it! Ugh, if Todd sees me driving little kids around, I'm gonna actually die of embarrassment."

"That's the famous Todd?" Barrie asked, straining to see the driver of the convertible.

Todd was Rita's major crush. He'd overheard his sister talking to her best friend, Brooke, about the guy. Not just talking—but *endless, nonstop analyzing* of Todd's every word and action from the school day for hours at a time.

Barrie had no idea how they could devote so much attention to the dude. Nothing they said made him seem even the least bit interesting or worthy of that much attention. But he did drive a cool car. Barrie could at least give him that.

"Get down!" Rita demanded.

John scooched as low as he could in his seat. "You can't die of embarrassment," he pointed out in his usual logical way. "That's physically impossible."

"Unless you're a *teenager*," Michael added with a shake of his head, tilting sideways below the window. "My older sisters are the exact same way."

"It must be like their Achilles' heel," Barrie said. "Like their biggest weakness—"

"Duck. Down. *Now*."

"Aye, aye, Captain!" Barrie said before diving as best he could on top of Michael. Once Rita was sure they were hidden, she rolled her window down. Barrie felt fresh air fill the car and heard the loud purring of the convertible's powerful engine.

"Uh . . . hey there, Todd." Rita giggled. "Nice ride."

Why did his sister—who was really smart—always sound so ditzy when she talked to her friends?

"Hey, Rita, what's up?" Todd said. His car rumbled with raw power. "You should come for a ride sometime. Maybe tomorrow night?"

"Interesting," Rita said, trying not to sound too excited. "Uh, lemme check my calendar."

Barrie rolled his eyes. He knew that she was just playing hard to get and trying to act busy to make Todd more interested. He'd heard her discuss her *Todd strategy* with Brooke endlessly.

"Okay, ready?" Barrie whispered to Michael and John, who both nodded.

"On the count of three," Barrie continued. *"One . . . two . . . three!"*

They all popped up from the back seat. "Boo!"

Rita jumped, dropping her phone.

Barrie pressed his face to the window and made kissing noises. "Oh, Todd . . . kiss me!" he cooed, smooching the glass.

Michael and John did the same, grabbing at each other playfully and pretending to kiss. "Oh, Todd . . . please be my boyfriend," they teased, giggling.

Todd cracked up. "Oh, no wonder you're so busy. Have fun babysitting!" Then he gunned the gas as the light turned green, and he took off.

Before the dust could even settle, Rita glared at Barrie.

"Goober, you're gonna pay for this!" she seethed. "You'd better sleep with one eye open from now on."

Then she drove on without saying another word. Her yelling was one thing, but the silent treatment was much scarier. Barrie had one thought as they closed in on their cul-de-sac.

Pirates are scary — but older sisters are worse.

3

THE JOLLY ROGER

"**W**atch your **step on** the gangplank!" the tour guide called from the front of the group. "It's a wee bit slippery."

Barrie stepped onto the gangplank, following Rita and his parents and the rest of their group—a mix of families and tourists. Waves sloshed under the unstable planks beneath his feet, and he fought to keep his balance, licking his lips. They tasted cold and briny. He felt like the ocean was surrounding him. It smelled . . . well . . . like something that was *alive*.

The pirate ship had its own special entrance separate from the main museum, which stood behind them. Barrie scanned the marina, taking in the rows upon rows of boats docked with their colorful assortment of names painted across their hulls. *Mermaid Lagoon. Skull Rock. Pirate's Booty.* Seagulls swooped overhead, peppering the clear skies and occasionally plunging into the water in search of a meal, while a few ducks bobbed on the whitecaps. Barrie eyed the dark, frothy water nervously.

What swims beneath those waves? he wondered.

Barrie wasn't afraid of much, but the open sea had always terrified him for some reason. Rita was scared of spiders, snakes, boogers, farts . . . and, well, just about anything she deemed *gross.*

But Barrie didn't mind any of that stuff. Spiders were pretty rad with all their eyes and legs and how they spun intricate webs out of nothing. He even thought that snakes were kind of adorable, much to his sister's abject horror.

And *everyone* knew farts and boogers were hilarious.

So, why did the ocean scare him so much?

Maybe it had something to do with that scary, old shark movie that Rita let him watch when he was way too young. He could still remember the creepy monotone music (*da-num, da-num, da-num*), the giant, slightly fake-looking shark cutting through the waves, and the tourists' feet dangling underwater, begging for the shark to chomp them off.

Maybe that's what happened to the pirate captain's hand, Barrie thought, staring at the water. *Maybe it was a shark's lunch.* He shuddered at the thought.

Anything could be lurking beneath that impenetrable surface, waiting for a chance to sink its teeth into him.

"What's up, Goober?" his sister asked, giving him a little push from behind.

It was only then that Barrie realized he'd stopped walking, frozen by his dire thoughts. Rita shoved past him, and Barrie took a breath, looking around. At the far end of the gangplank loomed the pirate ship. The words *Jolly Roger* were painted onto the side in ornate, cursive script, just like in the pictures online. The massive ship bobbed up and down on the unquiet sea. It looked even larger in real life.

A skull and crossbones flag flew across the bow, battered by the wind. The ship didn't appear friendly, but Barrie supposed that was the point. It was a pirate ship, after all. That flag had one clear message for any trespassers.

Stay away, matey—or else!

Distracted by the flag and its eerie skull symbol, Barrie felt his feet slip on the gangplank. Panicked, he wheeled his arms and grasped at the rope railing for support. The scratchy cord bit into his palms, burning them. The thin rope was the only thing keeping him from plunging overboard into the ocean.

Suddenly, a dark shadow in the water darted under the gangplank and came out the other side.

Faintly, he heard a strange ticking. He strained his ears, struggling to hear it over the waves.

Tick-tock. Tick-tock.

Was there a clock somewhere nearby? If so, where?

The shadow returned, slipping back toward the gangplank. Barrie's pulse began to thrum. Suddenly, a big wave sloshed up, spraying his face and stinging his eyes. He blinked hard to clear them, and when he looked back, the shadow was gone, along with the strange noise. He squinted at the murky water, trying to see beneath it, and listened harder.

Nothing.

Before he could ponder the mystery further, the tour guide's voice broke his concentration.

"Hurry up, mateys," the guy said, slipping into an awful cockney accent, like something out of a bad pirate movie. "No lollygagging on me ship—or I'll make ye swab the decks."

Barrie eyed their guide, a chipper local college student. *And also, clearly, kind of a dork,* Barrie thought, taking in his thick, unstylish glasses and stiff plaid shirt tucked into his high-waisted jeans. Who tucked their shirt into their jeans?

"*Nerd,*" Barrie muttered under his breath. He hurried the rest of the way up the gangplank, joining the rest of the group on the ship's deck.

Rita caught his eye and snort-laughed. "*Major* nerd," she whispered, making him giggle.

"Hey, be respectful," Dad said, shooting them both a chastising look. "And Rita, I expect you to set a better example for your little brother."

Barrie tried to stifle his giggles, but one glance at his sister sent them both into another laughing fit.

They didn't always agree, but at times like these, Barrie was reminded that they had way more in common than he liked to admit—especially when his sister was being annoying, which happened on a daily basis. Or more like an every-*minute* basis.

And nothing could bond them together like a dull history tour that their dad had foisted upon them. This wasn't the first time a perfectly great Sunday had been ruined this way. *And it won't be the last,* Barrie thought glumly as the guide launched into his boring spiel.

"Circle up and listen closely," the guide said. "You're standing on the deck of an *actual* pirate ship. We don't know how this ship survived—and in such great condition. Or where it came from. It simply showed up in the marina one day as if it appeared out of nowhere. But wow, aren't we the lucky ones!"

Or unlucky, Barrie thought, rolling his eyes at the guide's hokey theatrics. He knew they always embellished the stories on these tours. They had to, or nobody would ever sign up for them.

His father, of course, looked riveted, while his mother did her best to humor him and pay attention. Rita snapped her gum and fidgeted, clearly wanting to text Todd or Brooke.

"We're the only maritime museum in this area to have such a pristine pirate ship," the guide said, gesturing upward toward the masts. "And this one was captained by one of the most famous . . . or should I say *infamous* . . . pirates in history!" He let out a laugh. "Let's just say, you are in for a real treat! Now follow me."

Barrie followed the group as they descended the stairs to the interior deck. They stepped into a narrow, dark hallway, gathering around an oil painting that hung on the wall.

"I'd like you to meet," the guide said with great effect, "Captain James *Hook*."

The guide gestured to the painting. It was the same man Barrie had seen briefly on the museum's website. The captain looked regal in his crimson coat with its golden stitching, and up close, his hat looked even more imposing, adorned with its large white feather. The pirate had long, wavy black hair that cascaded over his shoulders, and he sported a thin black mustache that tapered to fine points, lending his face a menacing appearance. In his right hand, he gripped a scary-looking sword. His beady eyes seemed to stare directly at Barrie from above.

"You're standing on his ship," the guide went on, as the boat swayed under their feet. "And it's a good thing Captain Hook and his band of pirates aren't around to catch us down here—or he might make us walk the plank."

The group chuckled and muttered approving noises. Some snapped photos with their phones or fancy cameras, including his father. But Barrie just let out a bored sigh. *It's just a dumb old painting of a guy in a weird outfit.*

But even so, Barrie could not stop staring at one thing—the *hook* at the end of the pirate's left arm. Barrie couldn't help it. He raised his hand. The guide called on him.

"Yes, matey, got a question?" the guide said in his cockney accent.

"Uh . . . what happened to his hand?" Barrie asked, feeling self-conscious as everyone's eyes darted to him. "Is that why he's named . . . Captain *Hook*? Or did he choose a hook because his name was already Hook?"

"Great question, matey," the guide said. "We do

believe the name came after the Hook—that it's his pirate name, not his given name. Though we can't be sure. As for his hand, there are a few theories, but the truth is . . . we don't know. Sadly, that history has been lost. Your guess is as good as ours! It's one of our museum's greatest unsolved mysteries," the guide added with a fake grin.

Barrie's heart sank, disappointed. He was hoping for a more interesting, and hopefully gory, story for once.

Oblivious, Dad clapped his shoulder and flashed him a proud smile. "I knew you'd love this museum! I'm so glad we came for your birthday."

"Uh, thanks," Barrie forced out, along with a weak smile, trying not to think of all the fun his friends were probably having at the skate park today. That was their usual Sunday plan. It would have been way better than this lame tour. But then another thought occurred to him: *What if I can solve the mystery of Captain Hook and his missing hand?*

This could be his chance! A real shot at solving a real mystery, just like the kids in his detective books. *The Mystery of the Missing Hand.* It even sounded like some of the titles he'd read. Barrie loved sleuthing around, looking for clues. His heart thumped faster at the idea.

"Follow me," the guide said, leading them past a door with a sign on it.

KEEP OUT: CLOSED FOR RESTORATION

"That's Captain Hook's cabin," the guide went on in his cockney accent. "I wish I could show it to you, but it's currently being spiffed up by our staff. My apologies, but I promise to make up for it by delving into some serious maritime history. . . ."

As the group continued the rest of the way down the hall and back up the steps to the top deck, Barrie lingered behind, pretending to inspect the painting. But the truth was, he had other plans, and they didn't include listening to *serious maritime history*.

His eyes darted to the captain's cabin. This was his chance. He reached for the doorknob. He knew it was wrong to trespass, but he had one question seared into his brain. His eyes darted back to the painting—and the hook attached to the pirate captain's left arm.

How did he get the hook?

Maybe if he searched Hook's cabin, he could find a clue, something that others had missed. That's what the kid detectives in his books would do. They were twin brothers who solved mysteries together.

Barrie would have loved to have had a twin to go sleuthing with, but all he had was an annoying older sister. He chuckled just thinking about Rita in this situation. She would be exactly zero help.

But he knew what the brothers would do. After all, he'd read like a hundred of their books. They'd sneak away from the tour and search the boat for clues, just like he was doing. It was worth a shot, Barrie figured, and way more interesting than the dull tour. Plus, maybe he could solve one of history's greatest unsolved mysteries. That made his heart thump faster.

He twisted the doorknob. At first, it resisted, and his body heated up, leaving him wondering if he should just forget about it. But no. This could be huge! He put all his strength into his grip, and finally, the knob let out a creak and turned reluctantly. The heavy door swung inward, squealing on its hinges, revealing the dimly lit cabin.

SECOND STAR TO THE FRIGHT

Barrie's palms began to sweat. This wasn't the first time he'd snuck into a place where he didn't belong. When he played with Michael and John, they often acted out scenes from his mystery books and snuck into rooms where their parents didn't want them hanging out or random places they wanted to explore. But this was the first time he'd ignored a KEEP OUT sign. And this time, he was all alone.

Suddenly, the ship lurched under his feet as a big wave slammed into it.

Barrie staggered, then recovered. His stomach flipped. Yup, that confirmed it. He didn't like the ocean—not one bit. It was too unpredictable. It was too wild.

It was too much of everything.

Barrie slipped into the cabin, quickly shutting the door behind him. He felt a rush from disobeying the sign. His breath caught in his throat as he scanned the interior.

The cabin was surprisingly spacious, yet still cozy with dark wood floors and wall paneling that sloped upward, tapering toward the ceiling. The late afternoon sun filtered through the windows, casting shafts of light and shadows across the room.

As the sign had warned, the cabin was clearly under restoration. White tarps were draped over the walls, while tools and paint buckets were scattered across the floor.

Barrie took a few more steps into the cabin, taking it all in. In the back of the room was an imposing desk. He pulled the tarp off the desktop, revealing a polished mahogany surface that was covered with old maritime maps.

Barrie tried out the velvet-backed chair, sinking into it and peering at the desk. *Captain Hook once sat here*, he thought, scanning the parchment maps. He ran his fingers over the lines curving around the landmasses. He could feel that the maps were hand-drawn.

Through the windows, he could see the water spanning outward toward the horizon as if it had no end. Another thing he didn't like about the ocean. It was just too massive.

He imagined being out at sea for months in this rickety ship with only these old, paper maps to guide him back home safely—not even a phone or computer. That thought unsettled him.

He sat there, trying to imagine what the kid detectives

in his books would do. *Search the desk, of course,* he thought. He rifled through the drawers, looking for something that would help him solve the mystery of Hook's missing hand. But there was nothing other than old pamphlets for the museum, the odd pen, and lots of dust bunnies.

So much for that, he thought.

Out of the corner of his eye, he spotted a treasure chest in the back of the cabin, like something out of a pirate movie. *Bingo,* Barrie thought, jumping up and prying the clasp open.

Excitedly, he lifted the lid. Inside, it smelled like old wood and dust. He scanned the interior, and his face fell.

The chest was . . . *empty.*

Well, that's disappointing, he thought.

But of course the museum would have searched it already. Barrie dropped the lid.

Bang.

And that's when he saw them—scratch marks gouged into the floor, leading under the antique rug. His pulse skipped an excited beat, and his palms prickled. This was just like the stories in his mystery books, but even better because it was happening in real life.

What made those marks in the floor? And where do they lead?

Heart racing, Barrie rolled back the thick rug to reveal the bare floorboards. The rug was heavy, and the effort made his arms quiver. He grunted as he tried to push it aside. Out of nowhere, the temperature in the cabin seemed to drop. A sudden chill tore through Barrie, and he shivered fiercely.

He wrapped his arms around his chest to warm up, teeth chattering. Suddenly, he felt a breath on the back of his neck. Barrie's whole body seized with fear. No. Not possible. But there it was again. Another breath. Somebody was right behind him. Terrified, Barrie jerked around.

Nobody was there.

The cabin remained empty, but still, it felt impossibly cold. Outside, storm clouds had amassed in the skies, blocking the afternoon sunlight. Maybe that was it. A storm was blowing in from the ocean. But then he felt it again: warm breath tickling his neck.

"Wh-who's there?" he stammered, whipping around again.

But the cabin was empty. Silent.

Probably just the wind dropping the temperature and making strange noises, he thought uneasily. Or he was just being paranoid because he'd broken into a place where he wasn't allowed. He relaxed slightly and turned back. The newly exposed floorboards were darker because they hadn't been bleached by sunlight. The scratch marks continued over them, splinters jutting out from the deep gouges.

That's when his eyes fell on something that made his heart race even faster.

Hidden under the rug, he could just make out the outline of a secret panel set into the floor. The scratch marks stopped at the panel—but an X had been carved into the top of it.

Barrie knelt down to inspect the X, running his fingers over the crisscrossed scratches. *Just like in my mystery books*, he thought excitedly, *X marks the spot!*

There was a metal handle on the top. It looked antique and was in the shape of a skull and crossbones. What was hidden inside? Despite his heart thumping in his chest, he knew what he had to do. It was the same thing that the kid detectives in his books would do.

He reached for the handle to open it, holding his breath. His hand grasped the skull, feeling the metal eye sockets, and unlatched it. The secret panel screeched so loudly, Barrie was sure the nerd tour guide or some other worker was going to come running, but there was nothing.

No shouts or noise of rushing footsteps.

Only the slight rocking of the sea beneath the ship.

He breathed a sigh of relief. Carefully, Barrie reached into the opening and felt the outline of a wooden box. It was heavy, but he lifted it out. The box was old and covered in dust, but it looked fancy. Three initials were carved into the top: C.J.H.

Thump. Thump.

It sounded like footsteps behind him. Heavy ones.

Barrie glanced back in a panic, feeling his body tense. A breeze cut through the cabin, rustling the tarps and making them look like ghosts.

"Hello?"

No answer. The cabin remained empty. He strained his ears to listen and make sure. All he heard was the soft creaking of the ship as it rocked on the waves. Probably, it was just somebody walking on the top deck. Old ships like the *Jolly Roger* tended to make creepy noises. Probably.

Barrie turned back to the box. He unfastened the clasp and lifted the lid. The interior was lined with red velvet. His breath caught in his throat as his eyes fell on the object resting inside.

It was a rusty old hook.

4

HOOKED

Barrie stared at the rusty old hook, unable to believe his eyes.

I can't believe this is here, he thought. The hook was a huge clue, and *he'd* found it, just like the twin detectives in his books, only it was real. He lifted the hook from the box carefully, feeling how heavy it was in his hands. He touched the tip with his thumb.

"Ouch," he muttered, flinching back. Blood bloomed on his skin.

He stared at it in surprise.

The hook was still sharp, as if it hadn't aged a day, even though it had clearly been hidden down there for a long time.

How is that possible?

Thankfully, he'd had a tetanus shot last year after stabbing his toe on a rusty nail while playing in Michael's backyard, which was practically a homemade junkyard.

Did it actually belong to Captain Hook? Barrie wondered. He examined the initials carved into the top of the box again, feeling the deep indentations in the polished wood.

C.J.H.

"Captain James Hook," he whispered, remembering what the tour guide had said. *Unbelievable! How has this stayed hidden for so long?* He felt around the inside of the box for more clues. A corner of the velvet lining seemed to have come unglued from the box.

Strange, Barrie thought, sliding his fingers underneath it. They brushed something hidden behind the lining. Excited, he peeled the red velvet back more, exposing a piece of parchment paper. He pried the paper from the box. It looked like a secret letter. It was sealed with a red wax stamp.

He peeled off the wax stamp and unfolded the parchment. It looked old. Like super-duper old. His eyes scanned the ornate cursive.

I'M HIDING MY HOOK FROM THAT SCURVY BRAT. AS IF TAKING MY HAND WASN'T ENOUGH, NOW HE WANTS MY HOOK, TOO.

WHOEVER POSSESSES MY HOOK WILL HAVE THE POWER TO NEVER GROW UP.

KEEP IT SAFE UNTIL I FINALLY GET MY REVENGE ONE DAY.

—CAPTAIN JAMES HOOK

Chills rushed through Barrie from head to toe, bringing goose bumps to his skin. It did belong to Captain Hook. But who was the "scurvy brat"? Barrie didn't know. He scanned the letter again, rereading the part about "the power to never grow up."

"I could stay a kid forever," he whispered to himself, feeling his heart pump faster with excitement.

He thought about his upcoming twelfth birthday and elementary school graduation—and all the homework that he didn't want to do waiting for him at home. It was only going to get worse when he got to junior high school.

He remembered Rita and her recent sixteenth birthday, and how ever since then, their parents and her teachers kept piling more work and responsibility on her. Not to mention . . . *algebra*.

He still didn't know what that was exactly—only that it sounded horrible.

He also thought about his parents, who always seemed so stressed out about their jobs or worried about paying bills. Being an adult was *even* worse than being a teenager. The older you got, he realized, the harder everything became.

Barrie ran his finger over the hook, feeling the cold metal. Then he glanced at the letter again. It tempted him.

Never grow up.

But still, he hesitated. For starters, taking things that didn't belong to you was wrong. Not to mention this was a historical museum, which meant that the hook was a piece of that history. It belonged in a museum. What would his father think if he found out that his son had stolen a historical artifact?

Guilt pooled in his heart. He knew that it was wrong to take it—very, very wrong.

But none of that could temper his desire for his greatest wish.

"I want to stay a kid *forever*," Barrie whispered to the hook.

And it was true. That was what he most desired in this world. He glanced around the cabin to make sure that nobody was watching.

But the cabin was still empty. No one had come looking for him. He wondered if they'd even realized he was gone.

With a deep breath to steel his nerves, he slipped the hook, along with the letter, into his backpack and zipped it up—

Thump. Thump.

It sounded like heavy footsteps again. The ship rocked suddenly, and Barrie lurched forward. He stumbled to his knees and braced himself. *What* was *that?*

Out of the corner of his eye, he saw something move behind the tarps draped over the walls. The dark silhouette flashed past his vision. Barrie's stomach flipped.

For a split second, he thought he was in trouble and someone had caught him stealing the hook. But then he came to his senses. *It was probably just a wave hitting the ship,* he told himself, even though his heart was still jack-hammering in his chest. It must have made the tarps sway so that the shadows played a trick on his eyes. He was just seeing things again.

Taking a steadying breath, Barrie pulled his backpack on. The weight of the hook inside settled on his shoulders. A satisfied smile crept over his face.

He'd found a solution to his greatest problem. Now he never had to grow up.

But wait.

What if it doesn't work? What if this is just some prank?

Barrie hesitated. Should he put the hook back?

But then, worst-case scenario, Barrie would have a cool pirate hook to show off to his friends. And not just any hook—one that belonged to the *infamous* pirate captain. And he had the letter to prove it, so they'd have to believe him. Michael and John would totally geek out over the hook. They could play pirates in their secret Lost Boys hideout in Michael's backyard—

Thump. Thump.

That *noise*. The boat rocked under his feet. His stomach twisted. And then there was that shadow again, moving behind the tarps.

There . . . and then *gone*.

Barrie blinked hard and then stared at the wall. Nothing. Everything was still. It must have been his imagination. It tended to be overactive. Just ask his teachers. All the creepy pirate stories and being on a pirate ship could be messing with him, too.

Outside the windows, the sun was starting to set, casting the cabin into half darkness. He needed to get back soon, or his parents would start to worry. The tour was probably about to end, and soon the museum would close, too.

He turned to leave, but then—

Thump. Thump-thump.

This time it was unmistakably footsteps.

Heavy ones.

The cabin grew even colder, making him shiver. He spun around in a panic.

"Wh-who's there?" Barrie called out, even though

he knew nobody could be in the cabin with him. That would have been impossible. Surely, he would have heard the heavy door opening. The hinges squealed something awful.

He listened hard, but silence descended over the cabin again. He shook his head and chuckled to himself.

"Wow, I'm such a scaredy-cat," he muttered under his breath, thankful his friends weren't here to witness it. What would the twin detectives in his books think? But then—

Thump-thump. Thump-thump.

Barrie felt a rush of fear surge through him. He'd had enough. He had to get out of there. His heart hammering, he turned and bolted toward the door, fleeing from the strange noise.

5

SCURVY BRAT

arrie bolted from the cabin, slamming the door behind him.

Okay. You're okay, he told himself.

And then another warm breath hit his neck. Barrie backed slowly away from the door. What if it was Captain Hook? What if he was mad Barrie had taken his hook? But that was impossible. The pirate captain had to be long dead. Plus, Barrie was sure that the cabin had been empty when he entered it, and no one had come in.

Thump-thump. Thump-thump.

It was coming from *inside* the cabin.

Barrie's pulse thrummed in his ears. The ship felt even colder now.

SECOND STAR TO THE FRIGHT

Thump-thump. Thump-thump.

In a panic, Barrie turned and sprinted down the dark hallway, looking for the stairs. He was sure they'd been down this way, but he hit a dead end. He turned around and tried another hallway, but there was nothing down there except three more locked doors. He was trapped. Lightning flashed, lighting up the hall. He looked up— then jumped back in fear.

Out of the shadows, Captain Hook slashed at him with his sword.

"No, don't hurt me," Barrie yelped, jumping back. "I'll give the hook back!"

He cowered, expecting a hook to impale him. But nothing happened. Barrie cracked one eye open. It wasn't actually Captain Hook. Barrie was hovering under the oil painting from the tour. He let out a relieved breath, feeling foolish. In his panic, he'd thought the real pirate captain was here.

Captain Hook's beady eyes bored into him from his portrait. His lips curved back into a vicious snarl. *Give my hook back, ye scurvy brat!* he seemed to be thinking.

Barrie stared at the painting. Maybe he should put the

hook back, after all. He could feel the weight of it in his backpack and a sour feeling pooled in his stomach, making him feel slightly sick. Of course, the queasiness could have also been caused by the ship rocking on the ocean. The storm was churning up the waves, making it worse.

"Sorry, Captain—" he started to say to the painting. "I'll—"

But then, he heard the creaking of the door to the captain's cabin behind him, like it was swinging open of its own accord. The squeal cut through the hall.

Thump-thump. Thump-thump.

Barric's heart seized up. The footsteps were coming for him.

Blindly, he pivoted and found himself tripping up the stairs. The stairs! Once he got his bearings, he took them two at a time, climbing to the upper deck. The wood was slick, and he slid forward, almost face-planting. He caught himself only at the last second, barely avoiding a calamitous plunge overboard. His eyes cut to the plank that jutted out over the ocean. How many poor souls had lost their lives walking off it?

As he scanned the deck looking for the tour, the frigid

wind cut through him. The storm had intensified over-head. Raindrops pelted his face. But it was something more than that. It felt like someone—or *something*—was chasing him.

Something unnatural.

He remembered the warm breath on his neck in the captain's cabin. How every time he turned around, nothing was there. The strange shadows behind the tarps. The way the temperature seemed to drop suddenly. And where did that storm come from? That's when his mind jolted to his mystery books. They often featured haunted houses or haunted islands.

What if the pirate ship is haunted?

And if it was haunted, then it was probably . . . Captain Hook's ghost.

Barrie ran down the deck, passing close to the railing. Below, the ocean churned and frothed with great fury, splashing up against the hull and drenching the deck with salt water. Barrie could taste it on his tongue as he sprinted down the length of the ship.

He was looking for the tour or anyone to help him, but the ship appeared completely deserted. It was eerily silent, too, aside from the waves and the soft creaking of the wood.

Where is everyone? Where's my family? Where's the tour?

And that's when he heard it again—

Thump-thump. Thump-thump.

The footsteps were right behind him. He fled down the deck in a panic. Suddenly, the waves sloshed up, violently rocking the boat. He thought about jumping into the ocean just to escape. He glanced down at the waves, whipped into a frenzy by the storm's high winds. *Thump-thump. Thump-thump.* He leaned over the railing to jump. But then his ears pricked up.

Tick-tock. Tick-tock.

This new sound was coming from the ocean. The strange ticking echoed up from the dark water. Under the surface, a shadowy creature darted back and forth.

The ticking grew louder. If whatever was on the ship with him didn't get him, whatever was down there in the water would.

But then the strangest thing happened. Barrie started to feel warmer. The panic that had gripped him receded. Even the stormy skies seemed to quiet a little. Slowly, he turned around, staring at the empty deck. It was almost as if whatever had been chasing him had stopped.

Like it had evaporated into thin air.

Feeling uneasy, Barrie turned back to look at the water. How was that possible? Something had been chasing him. He'd been convinced. But now, standing alone as drizzle drifted down from the cloudy skies, he wasn't so sure. It was pretty dark out. Maybe hearing all those creepy pirate stories and finding the hook had sent his imagination into overdrive. Maybe his brain was messing with him. Even in his books, whenever a house was supposed to be haunted, the kid detectives always solved the mystery by the end, revealing that there was a real-life villain behind the "fake" ghost.

"None of this is *real*," Barrie whispered to the waves. "It can't be real. There's no such thing as ghosts."

He unzipped his backpack, half expecting the hook to be gone, too. But there it was, staring back at him, along with the parchment letter. He wasn't completely losing his mind. These things, at least, were real. But what about the rest of it?

He chewed his lower lip uncertainly. He didn't know

what to believe anymore. But staring at the rusty, old hook caused a fresh surge of guilt to wash through him. Maybe he should put it back, just to be safe? Whatever had just happened or not happened back there, it was wrong to steal the hook. That much was clear now. He had made a terrible mistake. He had to fix it.

Still feeling jittery, Barrie crept back toward the stairs that led down to the captain's cabin. His feet hit the wooden floor with a dull thud. The ship swayed uneasily under him. He glanced down into the thick darkness of the interior deck and listened closely for any sign of a presence, but there was only the soft creaking of the boat rocking gently on the water.

It wasn't real, Barrie thought. *It was just my imagination.*

Still, he needed to put the hook back where he found it. He needed to do the right thing. He started down the stairs, but then an angry voice growled through the ship.

"Where have you been, young man?"

6

TICK-TOCK

A dark shadow fell over Barrie from the top of the stairs.

"I'm sorry . . . I swear I was going to put it back!" Barrie raised his hands in fear, waiting for the slice of Captain Hook's sword.

"Barrie?"

He lowered his arms slowly. What he saw wasn't Captain Hook, but it might have been worse. His father stared at him from the upper deck. And he did not look happy.

"Put *what* back?" Dad said. His brows knit together, and his lips curved down into his signature disapproving-father expression. "Where have you been? We've been searching the ship everywhere for you."

"Uh . . . nothing. I mean, nowhere. I mean . . ." Barrie couldn't tell his dad that he had stolen something from the museum. "I guess I wanted to explore the ship on my own. And I got a little lost down here."

His father shook his head. "Barrie, you need to grow up and stop acting like a little kid already. I know how much you enjoy sleuthing, but you can't just wander off like that without telling anyone."

"Right, I'm really sorry," Barrie said, looking down in shame. "I just got really interested in Captain Hook. And I wanted to find out more about him."

It wasn't *exactly* the truth—but it wasn't a lie, either. He did sneak off to learn more about the pirate captain.

"Well, I can understand getting captivated by a piece of real history," Dad said. His angry expression evaporated. "Even so, your birthday is tomorrow. You're almost twelve years old now. You need to start taking responsibility for your actions."

"I will, I promise," Barrie said, relieved that his dad was softening. "I know you're right."

"Come on," Dad said. "Everyone's waiting for us by

the gangplank. Let's inform them that you didn't fall overboard."

He chuckled at his own bad dad joke. Even though Barrie still felt jittery, he forced out a laugh. As they headed through the ship, Barrie could feel the hook weighing down his backpack.

He glanced back at the stairs that led to the captain's cabin. He still wanted to put the hook back, but he couldn't risk letting his dad or anyone else find out that he stole an artifact from the museum. Especially when his father was already angry with him. Not to mention it was probably, like, a major crime. What had he been thinking?

There was no way he could fix it right now without getting caught. He'd have to put the hook back another time. With a sigh, he pulled his eyes off the stairs and followed his dad.

"Go apologize to your mother," Dad suggested as they headed back toward the tour group. "You really scared her. Even Rita was worried about you."

They approached Mom and Rita, who pulled a fake concerned face.

"Yeah, you shouldn't scare us like that," Rita said. "It's very uncool."

Barrie scowled. He *highly* doubted that Rita was worried about him. She loved putting on an act for their parents like she cared and was the perfect daughter when really, she'd probably be thrilled if he disappeared at sea.

Mom looked relieved. She hugged him fiercely, but then she went rigid. She stood up and crossed her arms, staring down at him. "You need to act more like your sister," she said, shuffling her purse to the other shoulder. "She knows better than to disappear like that."

Rita flashed a smug grin. She loved anything that made her look better than Barrie.

"Does that mean I get a later curfew?" Rita asked, trying to take advantage of the situation.

"We'll discuss it later," Dad said. "Now, let's hit the gift shop before they close. Barrie has taken a special liking to the pirate captain. Maybe I'll get him a little something extra for his birthday."

The last thing Barrie wanted was anything to do with pirates after the whole escapade on the ship, but he couldn't exactly say that, so he forced a smile. "Thanks, Dad. Sounds great."

Dad clapped his shoulder. "Bud, I knew you'd come around and like history, too. I'm so proud of you."

As they headed down the gangplank, Rita smirked and whispered, "Too bad you didn't really fall overboard, Goober, so I could get out of driving carpool."

That confirmed it. Rita was evil.

But before he could respond, the gangplank shuddered under his feet, jostled by a big wave. Barrie grasped at the rope railing, feeling his stomach flip. He glanced back at the ship. He could see the windows in the bow, and through them, the captain's cabin.

Suddenly, a shadow flashed past the window.

"Hey, did you see that?" Barrie gasped, pointing.

Rita rolled her eyes. "See what, Goober? The museum is closing. There's nobody on the ship."

"Over there . . . in the cabin," he said, pointing, but then he lowered his hand.

Whatever he saw—if he really did see something—was gone.

"I swear, there was something in the captain's cabin."

Barrie squinted at the ship. But the sun had almost set, and it was growing darker. "Like a ghost . . ."

He trailed off, realizing how lame that sounded.

"Jeez, you really are a child!" Rita said with an exasperated sigh. "Stop making up stupid stories and trying to scare me. That might work on your lame friends, but it won't work on me."

She tramped off, leaving him clinging to the railing with his heart thumping heavily in his chest.

Though he hated to admit it, his sister was right. He was acting super lame right now. Everyone knew there were no such things as ghosts. His eyes were playing tricks on him again.

What is wrong with me?

He had to get it together. He straightened up and sidled down the gangplank, trying to ignore the strange noise that now seemed to be following him. It was faint but unmistakable during the lulls when the waves receded, sucked back out to sea.

Tick-tock. Tick-tock.

The waves churned and receded; then he heard it again.

TICK-TOCK

Tick-tock. Tick-tock.

"It's not *real*," Barrie muttered, plugging his ears. "It's not *real*."

He glanced down at the dark, turbulent water. The sun had fully set now, and the water was opaque, but he knew that things lived down there.

Slimy things. *Dangerous* things. *Hungry* things.

But nothing that could make that noise.

I must be going crazy, he thought as he staggered off the gangplank and onto dry land. But even off the boat, the swaying of the ocean stayed with him, making him feel dizzy and nauseous the rest of the night.

It haunted him like a ghost.

* * *

After a hasty take-out pizza dinner with his family, since his parents were busy scrambling to get ready for the week at work, Barrie pretended to be tired and excused himself for bed. But really, he just wanted to be alone. He could feel the hook in his backpack calling to him.

"Good night, birthday boy," Dad said with a smile. He

was paying a big stack of bills on the kitchen table. "Get some rest for your big day tomorrow."

"Wow, I can't believe my little boy is turning *twelve*," Mom added from the kitchen, where she was pilfering another slice of pizza. "Where does the time go? You're almost all grown-up."

"Yeah, next year the goober will be a teenager," Rita snarked, looking up from her algebra textbook. "Freaky."

"Yeah, freaky," Mom agreed, picking off the pepperoni. "I remember when you could fit in my arms. Now look at you."

"Time sure flies," Dad agreed with a nostalgic chuckle.

"Don't worry, I'll pick up your cake tomorrow morning," Mom added, checking her lengthy to-do list on the whiteboard by the wall calendar. "So it's all ready for the party after school."

"Uh, thanks," Barrie said, backing away. "See you tomorrow."

The truth was, he wasn't sure how to feel about any of it. Well, besides the chocolate cake. He felt pretty good about that life choice. But he didn't want to grow up. His mom was right. It all happened so fast. He wasn't ready.

He left Rita at the kitchen table, agonizing over her algebra homework, and slipped into his bedroom. He shut the door, then set his backpack on his bed. His heart beat faster as he unzipped it and pulled out the hook, inspecting it more closely.

It was rusty and tarnished, but underneath the gunk, he could see a shimmer of silver metal. He ran his hands over the curve, testing the heft. The tip was still as sharp as ever. He was careful not to prick his finger again.

For fun, he slashed at the air with it, jumping on his bed.

"Stay back, mateys!" he said in his best pirate impression. "Ye don't want to mess with Captain Barrie!"

Then, he set the hook down on his pillow and pulled out the parchment paper. Careful not to tear it, he unfolded the letter and reread the cursive script.

Whoever possesses my hook will have the power to never grow up.

That's what I want, Barrie thought with a thrill. *I don't want to turn twelve.*

He waited for something to happen — some indication that the hook could grant his wish. Maybe it would glow. Or float. Or sparkle. But nothing happened.

The hook just sat there on his pillow.

Barrie sighed. He was an idiot for thinking it had any special powers. From the kitchen, he could hear his parents telling Rita to take out the trash before bed, followed by her usual complaints about too many chores. Then he heard her tramping up the stairs to bed.

Rap-rap.

He jerked his head up. His heart caught in his throat. Quickly, he tucked the hook under the pillow to hide it. He couldn't let anyone catch him with the stolen artifact. He grappled on the bookshelf by his bed for a book — *any* book — to pretend like he'd been reading. He found one, then flipped to a random page and propped the book up on his lap.

"Come in," he called out, trying to keep his voice steady.

Slowly, the door creaked open.

Rita poked her head in. She frowned at the book in his hands. It was . . . *Little Women*. He felt his cheeks burning. He'd never actually read it. The book was a hand-me-down from his sister, of course. And he pretty much never intended to read it.

"Thought you only liked mysteries?" Rita said suspiciously.

"Uh . . . it's assigned reading . . . for school," he stammered.

"Well, I won't keep you from your *little women*," Rita said with a chuckle. "But I just wanted to say—happy *almost* birthday, Goober."

"Uh, thanks," Barrie said with trepidation, waiting for her snarky comeback or her ulterior motive for being nice to reveal itself. But she just looked pensive. She bit her lower lip.

"You're lucky you're only turning *twelve*," she said with a weary sigh.

"Wait . . . what do you mean?" Barrie said, surprised. "You love birthdays. You were so excited for your sweet sixteen party, you couldn't stop talking about it."

And it was true. For practically a whole year, she'd

turned into a psychotic birthday princess and annoyed him—and anyone else unlucky enough to be in earshot.

"I *was* excited—past tense," Rita said as her shoulders sagged. She looked . . . haggard. "Listen, I thought it would be great, but it's not. It's like the complete and total opposite. I have more chores and homework than ever. I never have any free time. I'm always stressed out."

Barrie took that to heart. "Is it . . . *algebra*?"

Rita groaned. "Ugh, don't remind me. I've got an exam tomorrow. Exponential equations are gonna kill me."

"But what about getting your driver's license?" Barrie said. "Having a later curfew? Getting to go to parties? What about . . . Todd?" he added, unable to suppress a wicked grin.

"Please. I barely have time for my friends anymore," Rita complained.

"But you're always talking to them," Barrie pointed out. "And texting them. Like nonstop."

Her phone vibrated with a new text message as if proving Barrie's point. She pulled it out of her pocket and frowned at the screen.

"Yeah, it's relentless." She met his eyes, turning more serious. "Listen, it's school—but it's more than that," she confessed. "Like, I miss my old friends from when I was a kid. Remember Hannah and Jessie?"

"Yeah, what happened to them?" Barrie said. He'd noticed Rita didn't spend much time with them anymore, but he figured that she had a new group of cooler friends now that she was in high school. Not to mention her obsessive crush on Todd.

"Really, I don't know," Rita said with a sigh. "We used to be inseparable. We did everything together, remember? But when we got older, it's like we grew apart. We don't have the same interests anymore. We're not in the same classes. We're on different tracks."

"But what about Brooke?" Barrie said. "And well . . . Todd. You've got all these cool new friends."

Rita shook her head. "Yeah, but it's not the same. There's like all this crazy pressure to fit in and say the right thing," she confessed. "Look, you wouldn't understand. You're too young. I didn't get it either until it happened to me. I never felt that way around my old friends. I could just be myself with them."

under there. He was probably just hearing things again, he thought, annoyed at himself for being so jumpy. He was about to drift off back to sleep when, suddenly, he felt warm breath tickle the back of his neck.

He jolted upright, rigid with fear.

He scanned his room, but it was empty. Nobody was there. But it started to feel cold—*unnaturally* cold. His breath came out like fog, as if it was winter. And then he heard it again—

Thump. Thump.

The sound was definitely coming from under his bed. Something—or someone—was under there making that noise. Shivering, Barrie leaned over his bed to peer under it and squinted into the thick darkness. He couldn't see anything.

Blindly, he felt around under the bed, looking for the source of the noise. His fingers brushed dust bunnies, wrinkled comic books, a football, an old pizza crust. . . . *Ugh*. He really had to clean his room.

Then his fingers brushed metal.

Cold metal.

Terrified and barely breathing, Barrie moved his

fingers over the object. It curved around into the shape of a *hook*. He grasped it and pulled it out from under the bed.

It was Captain Hook's hook.

How did it get under the bed?

Barrie scanned his memory. He clearly remembered stashing it under his pillow after he made his wish. Maybe he accidentally knocked it off the bed in his sleep?

That was the only explanation.

Still feeling unsettled, he straightened up, clutching the hook. He listened closer, but the thumping noise was gone. He was probably hearing things. He shook his head. Everything was still. Everything was fine. He started to drift off again, when suddenly—

A shadowy hook slashed out at him from under the bed, whizzing by his ear.

Zing!

Barrie jumped back, holding the hook to his chest.

"What the—"

Another hook shot out. Then another. Then another. Barrie curled up against his headboard, trying to make himself smaller. The hooks slashed at him one by one, cutting through the air. Barrie dropped his hook and grabbed his pillow, holding it out in front of him for protection.

"Stop! Don't! Leave me alone!"

The hooks dug into the pillow, shredded the casing. Feathers rained down around him like confetti in the dim moonlight.

"It's a dream," Barrie whispered to himself, trembling. "It's just a dream."

Then, a large shadow slithered out from under the bed. The shadow grew taller and taller, forming into the shape of a man. He loomed over the foot of the bed and raised his left arm—the outline caught the moonlight.

It ended in a bloody stump.

Barrie blinked at the shadow. "C-C-Captain Hook?"

The shadow drew its sword. Barrie cowered back in fear.

"No, please don't hurt me!" Barrie pleaded. "I swear . . . I didn't mean to take it!"

But Hook raised his sword, aiming the tip right at Barrie's neck. "You're not the first scurvy brat to play a childish prank on me—but you will be the last," he sneered.

TICK-TOCK

"I'm sorry, I'll put it back!" Barrie begged, but Hook loomed over the bed.

"I shall have my revenge!"

His sword shot out at Barrie's neck.

7

NEVER GROW UP

Barrie woke with a start, clutching at his neck and gasping for breath. His heart hammered in his chest. Cold sweat slicked his skin. He felt as if he could still hear the thumping and feel the shadowy hooks slashing at him from under his bed.

The last thing he remembered was the sword stabbing at his neck and Hook's threats of revenge.

"It was just a bad dream," he whispered to himself. "It wasn't real."

The trip to the museum must have stirred up his dreams, transforming them into terrible nightmares. He sat up, taking a deep breath of relief. But then his eyes fell on something that made his heart hammer even harder.

His pillow was . . . shredded.

Feathers and ragged strips of fabric littered the comforter and floor. His mouth went dry. He reached down to touch the feathers and make sure they were real—that he wasn't imagining things—and something sharp dug into his palm.

"Ouch!" he yelped, yanking his hand back. Pain shot up his arm.

Barrie clutched his hand close to him as blood pooled in the palm. At first, he thought that Captain Hook was attacking him again. But then his eyes fell on the rusty hook hidden under the feathers. He'd pricked his hand on it.

As blood trickled down his arm, he struggled to make sense of everything. He must have grabbed the hook and shredded the pillow in his sleep, thrashing around from his nightmare.

He must have been haunted by his guilt over stealing the hook from the museum. That was the only way to explain the nightmares and his sleep-thrashing. He had to return the hook, and as soon as possible, even if it got him into trouble.

Looking around at the mess he'd made, Barrie felt silly *and* embarrassed. He was just glad nobody was around to witness it. Especially Rita. "Goober, scared of a stupid pirate ship?" she'd tease him relentlessly.

He'd never *ever* live it down.

He had to hide the evidence. After running to the bathroom for a bandage for his hand, he went back to his room and quickly swept the feathers up, tossing them in the trash. Then he stashed the hook along with the parchment letter into his backpack and zipped it closed. He was determined to do the right thing.

"I'll fix it," he promised himself, feeling better already. "I'll find a way to put the hook back." For the first time since touring the pirate ship, he almost felt back to normal.

That's when he remembered: *It's my birthday.* In the aftermath of the nightmare, he had almost forgotten. He glanced at the mirror, peering at his reflection. He was twelve years old now. He pressed at his chubby cheeks, then stuck out his tongue.

Well, he didn't look any different, and he certainly didn't feel any different. But he was definitely a year older.

On Friday, he'd be graduating from elementary school. Kindergarten felt like only yesterday, and now he was almost in junior high.

Time passed, no matter if you were ready for it or not. And it passed *fast*. Barrie's father was right. He wanted to hit the pause button—or better yet rewind—but that was impossible.

There's nothing to do except grow up, he thought, *whether I want to or not.*

Mournfully, Barrie glanced at his backpack. It had been ridiculous to believe that a rusty old hook had any power at all—let alone the power to stop him from growing up.

At least he'd get chocolate cake after school and time with his best friends doing what they loved most— hanging out at the skate park. And then tomorrow night, they were going to the Lost Boys concert. They'd been looking forward to it for months. That was a bright spot in all of this.

Despite his reservations, Barrie felt excitement swirl inside his chest. There would be a stack of presents waiting for him downstairs in the kitchen. And his mom always cooked his special birthday breakfast—chocolate chip pancakes. They were his childhood favorite. When he was a kid, he used to get to eat them all the time. Now they were reserved for special occasions.

Maybe growing up wasn't so bad after all. At least he'd get a party to celebrate it.

And chocolate. Lots of chocolate.

* * *

Barrie crinkled his nose up when he walked into the kitchen. His mother stood by the coffee maker, watching it percolate like her life depended on it. She looked even more tired than normal. Dad sat at the kitchen table with his tablet and a big stack of bills, while Rita was still struggling over the last problem in her algebra homework.

That was all perfectly normal. But there were no pancakes cooking on the stove. That was weird. There were also no presents piled on the kitchen table. Weirder yet, nobody greeted him with wishes of happy birthday.

Nobody even looked at him.

They were probably too distracted by work and homework and coffee making. His mother needed to down at least two cups to be functional. He just needed to remind them.

"I'm excited for my birthday party after school today," Barrie said in an enthusiastic voice. That should get their attention—he was never this cheerful so early. He reached over to pour himself some cereal. "I can't wait for my triple fudge cake after school—"

"What do you mean, honey?" Mom looked up from the coffeemaker and frowned.

"Yeah, what birthday party?" Dad said, looking over. He set his tablet down. "Oh, does one of your friends have a birthday today?"

"Uh . . . it's *my* birthday," Barrie said slowly. He stared at his parents, wondering if aliens had possessed them. "I'm turning twelve today. Don't you remember?"

He let out a chuckle, sure they were playing a trick on him. It was probably Rita's idea. But nobody else laughed.

"You know . . . 'cause that's what happens on your birthday," Barrie said, starting to get a weird feeling. "You turn a year older."

Now even Rita looked up with a concerned expression.

"Goober, it's not your birthday. You're still only eleven."

"Yeah, silly, it's not your birthday." His mother reached over to ruffle his hair.

Barrie stared at them in disbelief. It *had* to be a prank. They were good, too. They weren't breaking the act. He hurried over to the wall calendar, determined to prove them wrong.

He tapped on the square for today.

"Look . . . over here . . . on the calendar," Barrie said. "It says it's my birthday. . . ."

But then his voice dried up in his throat. The square for today was blank. Nothing was written there about his birthday. He was certain that it had been there only yesterday, complete with balloon drawings. He stared at the calendar in shock. It was like his birthday had been erased.

No, not erased.

That would leave some mark or sign behind.

It was as if it had never been written there in the first place.

"Uh, you can drop the act now," Barrie said, his pulse

beginning to race. He felt dizzy. "I get it. Nice prank. Very funny, Rita. Now, where did you hide my birthday presents?"

He started searching the kitchen for them, looking in the cabinets and rifling through the drawers. Then he peered under the kitchen table. But there were no presents.

His family watched him like he was going crazy.

"Prank?" Rita said. "You're clearly the one pranking us. Nice try trying to get extra presents out of the parental units. But I'm pretty sure it's not going to work."

"But it's not a trick," Barrie said, straightening up. He felt dizzy suddenly, like he'd just gotten off the Tilt-A-Whirl. "I swear it's true! It's my birthday. I'm turning twelve today. I'm having a birthday party after school with Michael and John at the skate park. Mom is getting me a triple fudge cake."

Dad shot him a weird look. "Kiddo, I hate to break it to you. But it's not your birthday. Are you feeling okay?"

"Honey, I'm pretty sure I'd remember the day you were born," Mom chimed in. "I am your mother, after all.

I was there when you came into this world. It was one of the best days of my life."

"Yeah, and I'd remember the day they brought you home from the hospital," Rita said in her best sarcastic voice. "And effectively ruined *my* life."

Barrie stared at them all in shock. Nothing in their expressions indicated that they were anything other than deadly serious. They really didn't remember his birthday. But how . . . ? Why . . . ? Out of nowhere, his stomach clenched. His eyes darted to his backpack, which held the hook.

It couldn't be.

Could it?

Did my wish come true? A hundred other questions rushed through his head, one after the other. *Does this mean I can stay a kid forever? And that I never have to grow up?*

"You're gonna be late for school," Mom said.

"Come on," Rita said with an eye roll. "Let's get you to kiddie school."

8

LOST BOYS FOREVER

"Seriously, nice try with that prank back there," Rita said, tossing her heavy backpack into the passenger seat. "Very convincing. You should consider an acting career."

"Uh, right. Totally." Barrie shivered as he climbed into the back, glancing at the cloudy sky. Even though it was almost summer, the weather was cold and drizzly, but that was typical in their New England coastal town. It didn't mean it would stay that way. The weather had multiple personalities. The day could go from cold and dreary to warm and sunny in the blink of an eye, then back again before nightfall.

Rita chuckled. "Trying to get presents, a cake, *and*

a party out of Mom and Dad? I gotta give you credit, Goober. Too bad you didn't pull it off."

"Yeah. It was a good one, huh?" He forced a laugh. His mind was still reeling, trying to process what was happening to him.

Rita sat behind the wheel and slid the key into the ignition, but she didn't start the engine. "You're lucky it's *not* your birthday," she said with a weary sigh, catching his eye in the rearview mirror. "Much better to stay a goober with minimal responsibilities."

With that, she started the car, shifted it into gear, and sped out of the driveway, heading for the other side of the cul-de-sac to pick up Michael and John. Their two-story brick houses loomed in the distance, as familiar as his own. Barrie had spent countless days playing video games in their bedrooms, or running around Michael's backyard inventing games of their own.

He remembered what Rita had said the night before about her old friends Hannah and Jessie—how they'd grown apart as they'd gotten older. Barrie would hate it if he wasn't best friends with Michael and John anymore. He couldn't imagine his life without them. They were the Lost Boys—nothing could tear them apart.

But hadn't Rita felt the same way about her friends? And look what had happened to them.

Okay, it was weird that his birthday had been erased. Disappointing and a little bit scary. But if his wish really was coming true . . .

He slipped his hand into his backpack, feeling the outline of the rusty hook tucked inside. Sure, he had been excited about the cake and party. But not having a party was a small price to pay if he didn't have to grow up after all.

I could stay a kid forever.

And better yet, he could keep his best friends.

Barrie spotted Michael and John together, tramping down Michael's driveway. They grinned when they saw him and executed their secret handshake.

Barrie couldn't wait to talk to them about everything that was happening to him. Even without a party, this was already the best day ever.

* * *

"Get lost, Goobers!" Rita said, dropping them off in front of their school.

"Love you, too," Barrie called back, knowing it would embarrass her. "See you after school."

She shot him a glare. "Don't remind me."

Then she sped out of the parking lot toward the high school across town. His friends cracked up.

"Your sis is nutso," John said, twirling his finger in the air near his temple. "But I think all girls are. It's probably the hormones. And all the hair products. There are major toxins in that stuff."

"Yeah, they don't make any sense," Michael agreed. "My three older sisters are the same way. It's like trying to understand an alien species that's addicted to dry shampoo."

Barrie cracked up, starting to feel almost normal. Kids streamed toward the old brick school building, a relic from the 1970s. The familiar sign read NEW LONDON ELEMENTARY SCHOOL. Barrie and his friends followed the crowd toward the front entrance, roving as their typical threesome. John was almost a head taller than Barrie and Michael now, and Barrie often wondered if he'd one day hit a growth spurt like that, too. He could still remember when the three of them had all been about the same height.

"Can't wait for summer break," Michael said. "Four more days until graduation."

"And then we're officially in junior high!" John added. He glanced at the first graders, who were half their height. "But until then, we can rule elementary school."

"Lost Boys forever!" they chanted together and executed their handshake.

Barrie took a deep breath, then asked the question he'd been meaning to blurt out since he and Rita had picked them up that morning.

"Uh, is there anything *special* about today?" he asked.

He wanted to make sure that his theory applied outside his home, and it wasn't just his family who had been brainwashed by aliens or something. His friends hadn't mentioned anything about his birthday yet, which was a sign for sure, but he had to be totally sure.

Michael frowned, thinking it over. Barrie waited, holding his breath.

"Are they dropping a new trailer?" Michael said, finally. "For the second season?"

He ran his hand through his choppy red hair. His backpack with the adorable baby alien from their favorite sci-fi show bounced on his shoulders as he walked.

"Oh, that's dope!" John said. "I can't wait. I'm gonna watch it like four hundred million times. Then I'm gonna read the heck out of Reddit threads for all the fan theories."

"No, it's not a trailer," Barrie prodded. "Anything else?"

When they didn't respond, he added, "Maybe something about . . . my twelfth birthday?"

John and Michael both shot him confused looks. They stopped in their tracks.

"Your birthday?" John said. "What are you even talking about?"

"You're still only eleven like us," Michael said. "Kids forever!"

"Yeah," John agreed. "We're your best friends. I'm pretty sure we'd know if it was your birthday."

"So you don't remember about my skate park party after school today?" Barrie asked.

"Uh, what kind of friends would we be if we forgot your birthday party?" John replied.

"Yeah, we're the Lost Boys," Michael added. "That's like the next level of friendship. Friendship version 2.0."

An awkward silence fell over their group. Michael and John both looked worried.

"Right, I'm just messing with you," Barrie said, backtracking and covering it up with a laugh.

"Ha, good one," Michael said with a chuckle. "You almost had me going there for a second."

"Yeah, I thought maybe aliens sucked out your brains through your nose and scrambled them up," John said with a giggle. "Like that freaky old horror movie." He pressed his nose flat and made a sucking noise like his brains were being extracted through his nostrils.

All three of them laughed.

Barrie really did have the two best friends in the whole wide world. And he wasn't going to let anything change that—even if it meant keeping the hook. He could feel it weighing down his backpack with each step.

"Don't forget to get a later curfew for tomorrow night," Michael said as they reached the entrance. "For the Lost Boys concert. No way I'm bailing before the encore."

"Oh, the concert!" Barrie said, feeling a rush of excitement. He couldn't wait to see his favorite band live with his friends. "I'm so excited. I'll make sure my parents remember about the curfew."

"Dude, I already got permission," John said, bopping his head. "My parents are all about me being in junior high. Freedom, baby!"

"I can't believe graduation is Friday," Michael said, shaking his head. "Next year is going to be so different. Changing classrooms all day. And we get different teachers for different subjects."

Barrie nodded, unsure how it would work with his wish. "Just as long as we don't have . . . *algebra*."

"Uh . . . what's that?" John asked.

"Exactly," Barrie said. "Trust me, you don't want to know."

Inside the school, the hallway was rowdy and filled with jovial chatter, even this early in the morning. All around them, kids bobbed and weaved through the packed corridor, heading for their classrooms, lest they miss the bell and get marked tardy. A gaggle of kindergartners bumped into them, acting silly and immature. Their shrill screams echoed through the hallway.

"Hey, watch it, Littles," Michael said, rolling his eyes. "Stupid goobers."

"Remember when that was us?" Barrie said, feeling a rush of nostalgia. He watched the five-year-olds cracking each other up with fart noises. That had been them once. So much had changed since then. Though, his friends still thought farts were funny. Who didn't?

"Yeah, much better to rule the school!" John added, scowling at the kindergartners and their silly antics. "At least for four more days."

They busted out their secret Lost Boys handshake as they reached their class. "Lost Boys forever!" they chanted together as they slid their hands apart and marched into the classroom.

Inside, Mr. Bates was trying to calm the raucous students and get them to settle down, but Barrie lingered back. He needed to examine the hook and letter. It was really happening—he didn't have a birthday today. Talking to his friends had confirmed that. They had never forgotten his birthday before. It could only mean one thing—his wish really was coming true.

"Hey, I gotta hit the bathroom," Barrie said, backing away. "I'll see you in a sec."

"Just don't be late," John warned. "Mr. Bates is kind of unhappy with you after last week and that whole not-doing-your-homework situation."

"Yeah, if you get marked tardy, there's no way your parents will let you go to the concert tomorrow night," Michael added. "You'll get grounded. Like for real."

* * *

Barrie knew it was risky—the bell would sound soon, and Michael was right about him needing to avoid getting in trouble if he wanted to go to the concert. But his heart raced with excitement over the thought that he had gotten his wish. That it had actually come true.

Now I can keep my friends, he thought, *and we can stay Lost Boys forever.*

His heart still pounding, Barrie closed the door behind

him. Across the hall, he spotted an empty classroom. The lights were off. It was a science lab. It was closer than the bathroom, which was all the way down the hall. He ducked inside the shadowy room. The overhead fluorescents were switched off. Stainless steel tables spanned the room. Metal shelves with beakers, microscopes, goggles, and other lab equipment lined the walls, along with slop sinks. EMERGENCY EYEWASH STATION read a green sign over the sinks.

Barrie checked to make sure the room was deserted. Outside, the halls had quieted down. He didn't have much time. Quickly, he pulled out the hook and letter from his backpack, ensuring that he still had them. As he ran his fingers over the hook and reread the letter, he felt elated.

"I'll never grow up because I don't have a birthday anymore," he whispered to the hook. "I'm going to stay the same age forever."

All his fears about getting older. The stuff Rita told him about. Losing her childhood best friends. The social pressure. And . . . *algebra*. His parents and their constant stress over their jobs and money and bills. Now he would never have to go through all of that.

He was always going to be a kid. No responsibilities. Just fun.

"Heck, I don't even have to pay attention in class anymore," Barrie whispered excitedly to the hook. He fished his math homework out of his backpack, balled it up, and tossed it in the trash by the eyewash station. "Good riddance." He already knew everything that he needed to be a kid. He didn't need to learn all that *boring* adult stuff. He'd never have to do algebra.

Drip. Drip. Drip.

Barrie tensed at the sound of rhythmic dripping. He glanced over at the eyewash station. The eyeholes were slowly releasing droplets of water. Somebody must have left the taps on. He turned them off, and they stopped dripping. He turned away, but then he heard it again.

Drip. Drip. Drip.

His breath caught in his throat. He was sure he'd turned the taps off. The dripping morphed into gushing. Slowly, he turned around. Water rushed out of the eyeholes. He leaned over the sink. The tap water smelled . . . like the ocean.

"That's weird," he whispered.

He tasted the droplets on his fingers. They tasted salty.

Quickly, he shut off the faucet again with an uneasy shudder.

Maybe they were having plumbing problems at the school? After all, it was an older building and run-down. Stuff always seemed to be breaking. He shrugged, zipped up his backpack with the hook, and headed for the door. He needed to get back to class before the bell.

Thump. Thump.

Barrie's heart all but stopped. It couldn't be. He froze in his tracks and listened harder.

Thump. Thump.

That sound. It was the same sound he'd heard on the pirate ship, but it was coming from the closet in the back of the science lab. Behind the glass of the door, he saw a shadow move.

Thump. Thump.

Heavy footsteps. They were unmistakable. Then he heard something else. It sounded like waves sloshing against a boat. He could even hear the creaking of wood.

Slowly, he turned around. The noises all seemed to be

coming from the eyewash station. The taps had turned back on again. Water gushed out and started filling up the sink. It overflowed onto the floor. Something was clogging the drain.

"H-hello?" he called out.

The water pooled around his sneakers and flooded the floor. He could hear and smell the ocean, even the faint cries of seagulls. How was that possible?

Slowly, he leaned over the basin, trying to see what was clogging the drain and causing the sink to back up like that. The water was murky and impossible to see through, just like the ocean. Pulse pounding, Barrie reached down into the sink, feeling around for the drain. The water swallowed his arm all the way up to the shoulder. It felt cold and smelled like the sea—brackish and alive.

His fingers snagged on something.

It was stuck to the drain, blocking it. It felt long and scraggly, like seaweed.

He retracted his arm, pulling it out of the sink. It was . . . hair. Long, curly, black. He kept pulling and pulling and pulling, and it kept coming out of the sink. Finally, he reached the end.

He held the matted clump of black hair in his trembling hands, staring at it in shock. How did the hair get into the sink? He was sure it hadn't been there before.

There must be a perfectly logical explanation, he decided. Just like the kid detectives in his books, he would find it. He just needed to investigate it. He turned back to the sink, which was still full of murky water, when suddenly—

A sword slashed out at his face.

9

HOOK'S REVENGE

The sword whizzed past his ear.

It just missed his neck.

But not by much.

Barrie didn't wait for the sword to stab at him again. He flung the gross, wet hair back into the sink, turned, grabbed his backpack, and bolted from the science lab, slamming the door behind him. The image of the sword slashing out of the sink kept replaying in his mind as he dashed down the hall, just trying to get away. His heart jackhammered in his chest. "It's not real," he whispered to himself. "It can't be real."

He sprinted with his backpack bouncing on his shoulders. The fluorescent lights beat down on him. The halls were deserted, and everything felt eerie and unsettling. Where was everyone?

And then he remembered—the final bell was about to ring. And he was running *away* from his classroom.

A new wave of panic crashed through him. He couldn't afford to be marked tardy. He turned around, his sneakers squeaking on the linoleum, and slammed right into somebody.

Actually, two somebodies.

"Whoa, watch where you're going!" Michael yelped when Barrie barreled into him, knocking him back into John. His two friends bumped heads.

"What's wrong?" John said, rubbing his forehead and grimacing in pain. "Uh, you look like you've seen a ghost."

"Dude, yeah," Michael added, eyes wide. "You haven't looked this freaked out since we made you watch that scary clown movie."

"And we all know the circus is your worst nightmare," John added with a snort. "Oh, and giant killer sharks. But that's Rita's fault. We do not accept the blame for that phobia."

Barrie stared at his friends in confusion. Their usual

banter felt out of place in the midst of his panic. He couldn't tell them the truth—that it was possible he had, in fact, seen a ghost. Of course, he knew ghosts weren't real. Even in his books, the brothers always ended up discovering the real explanation for the haunting. But he also couldn't explain what had happened in the lab.

At least, not yet.

"W-what're you doing out here?" he stammered. He still felt adrenaline coursing through his veins.

"Uh, looking for you, obvi," Michael said with a worried frown. "Don't want you to miss the bell. Or you won't be able to go to the concert. Your parents will ground you faster than you can say . . . *Never Land*." That was the hit single from the Lost Boys' first album.

"Yeah, we've gotta hurry," John said, tugging his arm. "It's about to ring any second."

Barrie followed his friends back to class. They dashed through the door right as the final bell rang. Mr. Bates shot them a chastising look from the front of the room. He'd scribbled a bunch of horrible-looking fraction problems on the board. They looked like a foreign language.

"Glad you could join us," Mr. Bates said with a scowl.

All the other students were already seated at their desks, ready for class. Barrie and his friends made a beeline for their three empty desks at the back. He could tell Mr. Bates was itching to mark them tardy. But they'd beat the bell and made it just in time.

"Uh, sorry," Barrie mumbled, taking his usual seat between Michael and John. He slumped lower in his seat, hoping to avoid further trouble. That had been close.

Too close.

As Mr. Bates launched into their first lesson—fractions—Barrie couldn't stop replaying what had happened in the science lab: the taps turning on by themselves; how the water smelled and sounded exactly like the ocean; the thumping noises coming from the closet; the long curly black hair clogging the drain; the sword stabbing at him from the sink.

He couldn't shake one terrifying thought, even though he knew it was impossible—*Captain Hook is haunting me.* It shot through his head, making his heart pound even harder.

But ghosts weren't real.

There has to be a logical explanation for all of this. I just need to search for more clues, he reassured himself.

The cases in his books all started the same way, with a haunted house or boat or island where it seemed like there was a real ghost terrorizing the inhabitants. But the kid sleuths always found a perfectly run-of-the-mill explanation that proved there wasn't actually a ghost or anything supernatural.

"Students, time to turn in your math homework," Mr. Bates said, pacing the aisles to collect it. Groans echoed out, accompanied by the rustling of paper as everyone pulled out their worksheets.

Math homework . . . oops.

Perhaps throwing away his assignment had been . . . premature.

Mr. Bates reached Barrie's desk and held out his hand. His shadow fell over Barrie.

"Uh . . . I don't have it," Barrie said, searching for an excuse, even a wild one, to explain. But his mind went completely blank. *I threw it away* simply wouldn't cut it.

Mr. Bates frowned. "Come see me at my desk, young man. We need to discuss this."

Michael and John shot him concerned looks. They'd both turned in their assignments.

That was it—Barrie was in big trouble. Now he'd never get to go to the concert tomorrow night. Mr. Bates was sure to call his parents and tell them. This was the second school day in a row that he didn't turn in his homework. He would get grounded for sure.

Uh-oh, John mouthed, dragging his finger across his neck. Michael just lowered his head. They both knew what this meant.

Feeling sick to his stomach, Barrie rose from his seat and followed Mr. Bates toward his desk. The class got started on the math problems that Mr. Bates had scrawled across the whiteboard. *Fractions.* They were awful. Though apparently algebra was worse.

"Look, I'm really sorry," Barrie said before Mr. Bates could say anything. He lowered his head in shame. "I don't have an excuse for why I didn't do it. Just go ahead and punish me. Call my parents. Send me to the principal's office. Do whatever you have to do."

Mr. Bates blinked at him. His eyes looked odd suddenly. Unfocused. "Punish you?" he said as if confused.

"Yeah, for not turning in my homework," Barrie said.

"Why would I punish you?" Mr. Bates said.

"Last week, I had to miss recess, remember?" Barrie said. "That's what happens when you don't turn in your homework. You get punished."

Mr. Bates glanced around, then lowered his voice. "Right, other *normal* kids get punished. But you're special. You don't need to do your homework."

"Wait, what?" Barrie whispered back.

"You're excused from all future assignments," the teacher said, still not quite looking Barrie in the eye. It was as if he was under a spell. "No more homework for you for the rest of the year."

"Wait, what do you mean?" Barrie said.

"Heck, instead of doing those boring math problems," Mr. Bates went on, "why don't you draw or play a fun game? How does that sound, kiddo?"

"You're serious?" Barrie stammered, unable to believe his ears. It was a dream come true.

No homework?

"Of course, you don't need to do schoolwork, either," Mr. Bates said, tapping his hands on his desk. "Since you're never going to grow up. You're excused from that as well. Just don't tell the other kids, okay? They might get jealous. It'll be our little secret."

Barrie stood there in shock. Had Mr. Bates really just said that out loud?

"Um . . . okay."

Barrie returned to his desk as his teacher blinked rapidly as if snapping out of his trance. Barrie's heart raced in excitement. This wish was even more powerful than he could have ever imagined. He'd expected that staying a kid forever would be amazing. But he didn't expect his teacher to excuse him from doing homework. Actually, not just homework—any and all schoolwork.

When the school day ended, Barrie hadn't done a single assignment. He had goofed off in the back of the room all day. He'd doodled cartoons in his notebook and played games on his phone while everyone else, including Michael and John, had worked hard on their lessons.

Right before the final bell, when Mr. Bates passed out their homework, he'd whisked right by Barrie's desk.

"Hey, wanna hit the skate park?" Barrie suggested with a grin as he and his friends gathered their things.

"Ugh, we've got so much homework," Michael said glumly, stuffing his papers in his bag.

"Fractions suck," John added.

"Come on, homework can wait—let's have some fun," Barrie said. "What do you say?"

Michael and John looked torn. Finally, they both smiled. "Lost Boys forever!" they cheered.

As they headed home to grab their skateboards and hit the park, Barrie could feel the hook's weight in his backpack. As long as he had it, he wouldn't have to grow up or do homework. Of course, ever since he'd taken it, some weird, creepy stuff had been happening to him. But there was probably a perfectly logical explanation for all of it, just like in his books.

He felt a stab of guilt. He knew he should still return the hook. It was wrong to take something that didn't belong to him. But then he thought about all the amazing things that were happening to him now that he didn't have a birthday. No homework? For the rest of the school year? It's not like he had to return it right away. It had been hidden for a long time, hadn't it?

As he skated with Michael and John down their street

toward the park, he felt a rush of excitement. He loved being a kid more than anything. He loved playing with his friends.

He was so glad he'd made that wish.

* * *

Barrie and his friends had so much fun at the skate park that they lost track of time. Barrie hurried home but still arrived after his curfew. His stomach twisted as he popped his skateboard into his hand and approached the front door, knowing his mom would not be happy.

The door opened before he even got there. *Gulp.*

"How's it going, kiddo?" his mother greeted him with a smile. She handed him a plate of homemade cookies and a sugary soda. "Have fun with your friends at the park?"

Barrie glanced at the clock, wondering if he'd gotten the time wrong. Nope. It was clearly after seven.

"Uh, great," Barrie said. "But won't this ruin my dinner?" he added hesitantly. Usually, she would never let him have cookies or soda on a weeknight.

Especially not right before dinner.

"Whatever do you mean?" Mom said, blinking. Just like his teacher earlier, she wasn't quite looking at him. "These are your two favorite treats! I baked the cookies just for you. Don't you want them?"

Barrie studied his mother, unable to believe what he was hearing.

This spell just keeps getting stronger, he realized.

"Thanks, Mom!" Greedily, he accepted the treats from his mother. It was almost too good to be true.

"What do you want for dinner?" Mom went on, setting her hands on her hips and smiling at him. "Mac and cheese? Chicken fingers? More cookies?"

She was listing off his favorite kiddie foods, which she never made him anymore. When he was younger and a picky eater, she'd make him separate meals. He'd get chicken nuggets and fries while everyone else ate grilled chicken and rice. But for the last couple of years, he'd had to eat what everyone else was having, including "healthier" adult foods like green vegetables that tasted like dirt . . . or vomit.

He couldn't believe his luck. His mouth watered at the prospect.

"All of the above?" he ventured.

He still expected her to change her mind. Or make him pick one option.

"Sure thing!" Mom said in a cheery voice without missing a beat. She walked briskly into the kitchen, pulling out the mac and cheese box—his favorite kind with the fluorescent orange powder. "Anything for my favorite little guy."

"What about ice cream, too?"

He knew he was pushing his luck, but he had to try.

"Of course!" Mom said looking up with a warm smile. "Chocolate? Better yet, I won't make you wait until after dinner to eat it. Why don't you have some right now?"

Best day ever!

Giddy, Barrie started to set the table—his usual chore before dinner.

But his mother shot him a confused look.

"You don't need to do that," she said, her eyes still unfocused. "It's your sister's job to set the table, remember? Why don't you go watch cartoons until it's dinnertime?"

Barrie broke into an evil grin. That's right—Rita could do his chores. She was all grown up, after all.

He settled into the sofa and flipped on his favorite sci-fi cartoon with the baby alien and the space wizards. As the robots beeped and blipped across the screen, chasing the alien, he sipped his soda and munched on the cookies, feeling the grainy sugar coat his tongue. His mother dropped off a heaping bowl of chocolate ice cream, which he ate all the way to the last bite.

Dinner went even better than expected. He got mac and cheese with cartoon-shaped noodles, crispy chicken fingers with ranch dressing and barbecue sauce, more cookies, *and* chocolate ice cream. Plus, soda to wash it all down. It was the single best meal of his life. Everyone else had to eat dry chicken breast, brown rice . . . and *spinach*.

Barrie couldn't fathom how leaves were considered an actual food. They were inedible. Rita seemed to share his sentiment, pushing the spinach around her plate unhappily. She kept shooting him jealous glances.

"Rita, eat your veggies," Mom said. "You're sixteen now. Start acting like it. They have important nutrients."

She pouted. "Ugh, can't I just take a vitamin? It's like science. You love science."

"Your mother worked hard to make dinner," Dad

said. "And we both worked hard to pay for it. Stop complaining. You're too old for that."

"Why doesn't Barrie have to eat spinach?" she said, shooting him a spiteful look.

"Your brother's still just a kid," Mom said. "You know that. You're sixteen. Soon you'll be in college. It's time for you to grow up."

"That's right," Barrie said, shooting her an evil grin. "Eat your veggies."

Rita glared at him, taking a grudging bite of spinach and grimacing at the acrid taste.

If looks could kill, he'd probably have dropped dead on the spot. But Barrie didn't care. He just grinned at her and stuffed another cookie in his mouth. He ate until everything was gone. Mom even let him have another serving of chocolate ice cream. He wolfed it down, savoring the rich sweetness.

As he slipped into bed after playing video games for hours, he was certain that this had been the single best day of his life—even if he hadn't gotten to have his birthday party and his triple fudge cake. Staying a kid was the best thing that had ever happened to him.

* * *

Scratch. Scratch. Scratch.

Barrie woke with a start. It was dark outside. He sat up in bed, his mouth clammy from all the sugar he'd had earlier. He felt exhausted, and his brain felt foggy. He had stayed up much later than normal for a school night.

Barrie rubbed his eyes, letting them adjust—then he gasped at what he saw above his bed.

Slash marks were gouged into the ceiling in a jagged X pattern.

Barrie stared at them in shock. Feeling his heart pounding, he stood up on his bed and reached his hand out. He ran his fingers over the slash marks. They were deep.

And they were very real.

Scratch. Scratch. Scratch.

There was that sound again—coming from under the bed, like something was scratching at the floorboards. *It's just another nightmare*, he thought groggily. *None of this is real*. His head was thick with sleep. He had a serious sugar hangover. Hadn't he read somewhere that too much sugar could act almost like a drug? It could probably make you hallucinate if you had too much of it. Maybe the third helping of ice cream wasn't the wisest choice.

I'll just have two next time, he promised himself.

As if hearing his thoughts, the noise stopped abruptly. Slowly, Barrie leaned over to peer under the bed. He gazed into the thick darkness but saw nothing. Just blackness.

"Hello . . . is someone there?" he whispered.

He held his breath and stared, squinting in the dark.

The last thing he saw was a flash of silver aimed right at his face.

10

MAJOR FOMO

Barrie jumped back and flipped on the lights.

There was nothing. No sword. Nothing.

He gasped for breath, scanning his room for any sign of something out of place. For someone who could have been wielding the sword that he'd been sure was there just seconds ago. But he was alone. Relief washed over him; it was just a nightmare. He slumped back on his bed, trying to slow his racing heart.

And that's when he saw it—the slash marks in the ceiling.

His heart jumped into his throat. The gouges were still there. So . . . not a dream, then. He stood up and reached for the slash marks again, hoping that he was seeing things.

But the gouges were rough beneath his fingertips. They really were real.

Cautiously, Barrie checked under his bed once more. Deep slashes had been gouged into the wooden floorboards there, too. Splinters and specks of wood stuck out of the gashes. He studied them, unable to believe his eyes.

"This can't be happening," he whispered.

The slashes looked exactly like the ones he'd discovered on the pirate ship in the captain's cabin. Those marks had led him to the secret compartment where he had discovered the hook and the letter.

Oh no, the hook!

Barrie scrambled over to his backpack: a gash had been slashed into its side. The rough fabric—which he had thought of as indestructible—gaped open.

It was almost like someone—or *something*—had been searching his room for the hook. He reached inside, certain that the hook had been taken. But it was still nestled in there, along with the parchment letter. His heart rate slowed, but only slightly.

Why didn't they take it?

Barrie must have woken up and surprised them. That was the only explanation. That's why they hid under his bed. He pulled the hook out and stroked it, remembering how amazing yesterday had been. He never wanted it to end. He never wanted to grow up.

He had to keep this hook at all costs.

He studied the slashes over his bed and the gash in his backpack. Had someone really been in his room, looking for the hook? He could think of only one person who would want it back—one person who could make those marks on the ceiling and floor.

Captain Hook.

Barrie felt the cold metal of the rusty hook, running his finger to the sharp tip.

"But I need this," he whispered. "You can't have it back. I can't grow up."

* * *

"No, you're not allowed to go to the concert tonight," Mom said, downing her usual supersized mug of morning coffee.

"Wait, what? What do you mean?" Barrie demanded.

Mr. Bates had excused him from homework for the rest of the school year. He wasn't in trouble—at least any that he knew about. He wasn't currently grounded, which was basically a minor miracle since he tended to get grounded a lot. There was zero reason that he shouldn't be allowed to go to the concert. They'd already given permission and bought the ticket for him.

"Exactly what I said," Mom repeated in a tired voice. "You can't go tonight."

"But why not?" Barrie gasped. "You bought that ticket for my birthday, and I . . ."

The words dried up in his throat.

The birthday that never happened because of his wish.

"For starters, you're too *young* for concerts," Mom said, pouring a fresh cup of coffee and sipping it black. "I spoke to your father last night. We both agreed. You would need adult supervision, and neither of us can go. Also, it will end way past your curfew. We never should've bought you the ticket."

"But everyone else is going," Barrie said. "Michael's

and John's parents gave them permission. It's our favorite band. We've been looking forward to it for months."

Mom let out a weary sigh and set her empty mug in the sink.

"That's *their* parents," she said, spouting one of her favorite parenting lines. "We're *your* parents. We have different rules in this house. We've decided to give your ticket to Rita."

"No way!" Barrie gasped. "Why does she get to go?"

Rita shot him a snarky look from the kitchen table, where she was furiously finishing her homework. "Yeah, Goober," she said, stabbing her pen in the air to emphasize her words. "Different rules means *I* get to go to the concert tonight."

Barrie couldn't believe the unfairness. His mouth dropped open in outrage.

"But why does Rita get to go?" he asked again in a whiny voice. He hated sounding like a little kid, but he couldn't help it. "That's totally unfair! It's my ticket! She can't have it—"

"Because she's all grown up," Mom replied, rubbing her tired eyes. "She's sixteen. She can drive, and she gets a later curfew. Plus, it's not *your* ticket. Your father and I paid for it—"

"But she can give me a ride," Barrie said, thinking fast. "We'll get another ticket so we can both go. And she can supervise me. She's babysat me before—"

"No way, Goober," Rita said. "I need a night off from you and your lame friends. Plus, the concert is totally sold out. Brooke told me. No way can we score another ticket."

Dad walked into the kitchen with his messenger bag slung over his shoulder. He was ready for work. He met Barrie's eyes. "Son, I'm sorry, but you're just too young for concerts," he said, patting Barrie's shoulder. "Don't argue with your mother. You know better than that."

"But I really wanted to go," Barrie said, blinking back angry tears. He couldn't stand how unfair it all was. "I can't believe you're letting Rita go instead of me! They're my favorite band. She doesn't even like them that much. All my friends are going—and half my class."

Dad gave him a sympathetic look. "If your friends all jumped off a cliff, would you jump, too? Just because everyone else is doing it doesn't mean you should, too."

He chuckled at his own lame dad joke. Barrie just

scowled back, feeling even worse. This was yet another lame parenting line that he'd heard a gazillion times before. Going to a fun concert was *not* the same thing as jumping off a cliff. It made zero sense.

"But I'm gonna miss out," Barrie said, imagining Michael and John at the concert without him, jumping around and singing along. Then his father perked up.

"Oh, I know!" Dad said. "How about I take you to the children's museum instead? That's more age appropriate."

"Yes, that's a fantastic idea," Mom said with a nod. "It's also . . . educational."

Barrie cringed at that word. He stared at them both in horror. They were just making it worse. Why did his father think that museums were the answer to every single life problem?

And not just *any* museum.

The children's museum.

That was like the most boring place in existence. Not to mention it was for snotty little kids who were still in diapers. At least the maritime museum had a pirate ship and other semi-cool stuff.

He felt his heart sinking. The Lost Boys were his

absolute favorite band. He knew every song by heart. The chorus from his favorite song, "Never Land," ran through his head. It played on the radio constantly.

> *The sky's the limit,*
> *Never grow up, never get older!*
> *Second star to the right,*
> *And straight on till morning.*

He'd been looking forward to going to the show with his friends for so long. He couldn't believe he was going to miss it.

He studied his parents' faces for any glimmer of hope that their resolve was weakening and he could convince them, but they looked firm. He could tell from experience. They weren't going to change their minds, not once they'd made them up like this.

Feeling defeated, Barrie followed Rita out the door, grabbing his backpack with the gash in the side. It was time for school. They climbed into the car and he slumped in the back seat. He was dreading telling Michael and John the news that he couldn't go. They did *everything* together.

"Enjoy the kiddie museum, Goober," Rita smirked as if reading his mind. "Meanwhile, I'll be rocking out with my friends."

She made the *rock out* symbol with her hands and fired up "Never Land." The song blared from the speakers, making Barrie feel even worse—which he hadn't thought possible.

"You don't gotta rub it in," Barrie mumbled, feeling like a dagger had been plunged into his heart.

Rita glanced in the rearview mirror. He could tell she wanted to do just that, but then she spotted the desolate expression on his face and softened.

"Hey, cheer up," she said. "I'll send you vids from the show."

But he didn't want videos—he wanted to be there with his friends and the cool kids. He couldn't believe that Michael and John were going to see the Lost Boys without him.

His mother's words ran through his head again: *You're too young for concerts.*

It just wasn't fair.

He reached into his backpack through the gash in

the side, feeling the outline of the hook. He was sure that the wish had caused this to happen. That was the only possible explanation for why his parents would suddenly decide that he was too young for a concert. For the first time, as he slumped in the back seat listening to his favorite song, he started to wonder if not growing up was such a good idea after all.

* * *

The children's museum was even worse than he expected.

All the exhibits were overrun with snotty little kids wired on sugar or adrenaline—or maybe both. They careened around the museum like drunken sailors, bumping into each other, squealing in shrill voices, and smearing their sticky hands everywhere.

Barrie was definitely the oldest kid there. When he was younger, he'd loved this museum, especially the ocean exhibit, where they let the kids pick up starfish. But now, as he surveyed the colorful, geometric designs and oversized signs, he felt like he didn't belong. *I should be at the concert with my friends,* he thought glumly, *not stuck here with these little brats.*

"Go have fun with the other kids," Mom said, oblivious to his sour mood. Her eyes had that glazed-over look. "I'll be over here if you need anything."

She joined a gaggle of parents clustered by the hard plastic chairs. They all seemed absorbed in their phones, as if they'd rather be anywhere else. Barrie could relate—he felt the exact same way.

He meandered through the museum, looking for a group of kids that he could join, but none of them looked fun. He was a few years older than everyone there.

Buzz. Buzz.

His phone vibrated in his pocket and he fished it out, opening to his messages. He hit play on a video Michael had sent him. The screen flooded with an image of John up close, with the brightly lit stage in the background.

"Wish you were here!" John yelled before tilting the lens toward the stage, right as the band launched into "Second Star." Colorful lights swirled around while backup dancers rocked out. Star-shaped spotlights roved over the packed crowd, who were bouncing around and looked like they were having the time of their lives. "*You're the* second *star I see every night, but of all the stars, the brightest light,"* the trio sang in perfect harmony while playing their instruments. *"Never stop flying, never grow up, dreams are forever, and childhood doesn't stop."*

Barrie felt his mouth go dry. Envy rose up in him like a poisonous tide. Rita sent him a video, too, as promised. She was there with Brooke and Todd. It seemed like her painstaking plans to get Todd's attention had worked. Todd had his arms wrapped around Rita.

Yuck, Barrie thought, imagining them making out during the show.

Barrie played and then replayed the videos over and over, feeling worse every time he watched them. Suddenly, staying a kid didn't seem so fun after all. He missed his friends. He had missed the concert.

Did I make a huge mistake?

He wandered over to the ocean exhibit—his former favorite—passing through a shadowy corridor painted blue and designed to emulate the sensation of being underwater. Facts about undersea life were painted across the walls in colorful script, along with fanciful sea images.

He reached the end of the corridor. Strangely, the exhibit was dark, except for the open tank of water in the middle. Eerie blue light filtered through the salt water, casting strange, rippling shadows across the walls and ceiling. It really did feel like being underwater.

It was also deserted. This was strange. In the past, there had always been dozens of little kids running around the exhibit, splashing in the water and harassing the starfish. For half a second, Barrie felt relieved to have the room to himself, but then he heard it behind him—

Thump. Thump.

Barrie tensed. He whipped around, but he was completely, utterly alone.

He strained his ears.

The room was eerily silent, aside from the burbling of the tank. He felt cold suddenly and shivered in his light T-shirt. But museums were usually kept on the colder side, weren't they?

Barrie approached the tank. Wrapping his arms around his chest, he peered down into the water, but only harmless starfish lay on the sand, clustered around the coral reef. He reached his fingers in and stroked one of them, feeling the bumpy surface. This exhibit had always soothed him, ever since he was a little kid. While he was scared of the ocean, this felt contained and safe. He could see the bottom. The water was clear. It contained only harmless creatures.

Then, suddenly, an eerie voice reverberated out of the water.

"Scurvy brat!" the voice gurgled, sounding deeply furious. "You're not the first little boy to take something from me that doesn't belong to you—but you will be the last!"

11

HOOK'S GHOST

Barrie bolted down the corridor. His heart felt like it might jump out of this chest.

He could still hear the threatening voice booming out of the water at him. *Scurvy brat!* For the first time, he knew what he'd heard. He was wide awake this time. It wasn't just a dream. And it wasn't his overactive imagination, either. There was no mistaking that voice.

It's Captain Hook. He's after me, Barrie thought wildly.

But there was no way that the pirate was still alive. His pirate ship was in a museum. Which could mean only one thing: Captain Hook's ghost must be haunting him, and had been ever since he stole the hook from his ship.

That would explain all the weird things that had been happening to him since that day.

He knew, on the one hand, that ghosts didn't exist. But on the other hand, he knew that the hook had magical powers. It had granted his wish to never grow up, hadn't it? So wasn't it possible that Captain Hook's ghost was real, too?

It sure felt real. And it was clearly furious at Barrie for stealing his hook. *You're not the first little boy to take something from me that doesn't belong to you — but you will the last!*

The words echoed through his head again, making Barrie's heart almost explode with fear. He cut through the museum, running as fast as he could to get away from the ocean exhibit, down the dark and shadowy hall. He kept expecting Captain Hook to leap out of the darkness and attack him. Every shadow looked like a threat.

Finally, he burst back into the main exhibition hall. Here, it was brightly lit and there were kids everywhere. He found his mother glued to her phone, along with the other parents. They all looked tired and vaguely annoyed by their offspring running all around the museum.

"Mom . . . he's here!" Barrie panted in a panicked

voice. Now that he knew Hook's ghost was really haunting him, he had to get help. "We're in real danger! We have to go!"

"Who's here, sweetie?" Mom said, looking up from her screen. She had a glazed-over look in her eyes. "What're you talking about? Slow down and speak clearly."

"Captain Hook . . . his ghost . . . he's after me . . ." Barrie started, but the words dried up in his throat the second he said them.

He realized how crazy he sounded.

A second ago, he didn't believe in ghosts, either. But he knew what he'd heard back there. And he knew that Captain Hook's ghost was really after him.

"Oh, that's just your overactive imagination," Mom said with a weary sigh. She bent down and patted his head to calm him down. "You know how you get those bad dreams."

The other parents looked over and chuckled knowingly.

"My little Bobby still can't sleep without a nightlight," one father said with a smile. "He thinks monsters live under his bed."

The parents all laughed in commiseration. Barrie's cheeks burned.

"But I swear . . . he's real!" he protested. "It wasn't a dream—I was wide awake. He's been haunting me ever since we went to the maritime museum—"

"Sweetie, pirates aren't real," Mom said slowly, like she was talking to a little kid. "You know that. At least, not anymore."

"But he is real!" Barrie said in an urgent voice. "It's gotta be his ghost. That's the only explanation—"

"Listen, I told your father it was a bad idea to take you to that pirate ship," Mom said with a weary sigh. "But we thought you were old enough to handle it."

"Mom, I swear . . . Captain Hook's ghost is haunting me," Barrie pleaded. "You have to believe me. And he's mad at me. . . . He wants to hurt me."

But she just shook her head and grabbed his hand. "Come on, sweetie, let's get you home for bed. Wow, I'm sure glad we didn't let you go to that concert! Clearly, you're not old enough for that if you can't even handle a trip to the children's museum."

Barrie wanted to protest further. He wanted to argue

that he wasn't seeing things. That Captain Hook's ghost was really haunting him. Maybe he could show her the hook and the note that he stole from the ship? But then he caught himself. He couldn't show those things to his mom—then she'd know he was a thief on top of everything else.

As they drove toward home, taking the familiar route by the sea, Barrie started to feel even worse. His phone kept vibrating with new texts from his friends, but he switched it off. He knew they were having the best time of their lives—and he was missing it. FOMO had never felt so strong. It stung at him like needles poking at his brain.

He stared out at the black waves, replaying everything from the last few days in his head. At first, not growing up had seemed so great, but it was quickly turning into a nightmare. Not getting to go to the concert was bad enough, but now Hook's ghost was after him, too.

How could he make it stop?

They pulled up to the house, got out of the car, and were heading for the front door when Barrie skidded to a halt in his tracks.

"Oh no!" he gasped, flinching back from the door. "Watch out!"

The front door had been slashed. Deep gouges scoured the wood. Paint flecks and splinters littered the doorstep. Two words had been hacked into the wood in jagged letters, but they were unmistakable.

SCURVY BRAT

His mother eyed him, confused. "What's wrong?"

"Uh, can't you see it?" he said, aiming one shaky finger at the message. "It's like right there."

Mom squinted at the door.

"Oh, this?" She bent down to scoop up a pamphlet that had been shoved into the doorframe. It was an ad for a local tree-trimming service. "Just those solicitors who keep pestering us. Nothing to worry about."

She crumpled up the pamphlet, slid her key into the lock, and unbolted it. Then, she thrust the front door wide open and swept inside as if nothing were amiss.

Why couldn't his mother see it?

Barrie just stared at the door in shock. The

message—*SCURVY BRAT*—stared back at him. It was clearly there, plain as day. Another terrible thought occurred to him.

Was his family in danger, too? What was he going to do?

* * *

"Jeez, you're awful jumpy today," Michael said as they walked into school on Friday morning. He shot Barrie a concerned look. "What's gotten into you? I mean, you're usually a total weirdo, but this is worse than normal."

Barrie had dark circles under his eyes and could barely keep them open. He had tried to stay up all night for the last two days. Every time he fell asleep, terrible nightmares haunted him—nightmares that might have been real. Swords slashed out of the darkness at him. He'd wake up with his heart pounding, often to new gashes on the ceiling or in the headboard of his bed. Every shadow made him jump. He was growing increasingly jittery with every day that passed.

Hook's ghost wasn't letting up.

Barrie was sure it was the captain's ghost now, even

if that sounded crazy. The encounter at the children's museum had confirmed it. If he didn't find a way to make it stop, he was going to lose his mind.

"Yeah, has Rita been even more freaky than normal?" John asked with a snort.

"Uh, yeah," Barrie said, distracted. Part of him wanted to tell Michael and John what was going on, but a bigger part of him feared that his friends wouldn't believe him. "My sister's a total freak and a half."

He scanned the shadows in the corners of the hallway, half expecting a sword to lash out at him, or that voice to boom out. He couldn't get it out of his head.

"Did you hear they're going to release the concert from the other night on streaming?" Michael said, making Barrie jump. He broke into an air guitar solo, dropping to his knees. "Now you'll get to see the whole thing."

"Oh, yeah?" Barrie said vacantly.

"Yeah, it was so lame you couldn't go," John said. "But I saw your sister making out with that loser Todd." He made a grossed-out face like he was sucking a lemon. "So at least you didn't have to witness that crime against humanity."

Barrie started toward their classroom, but Michael shot him a weird look.

"Hey, where're you going?" he asked. "Did you forget about today?"

"What do you mean?" Barrie said, skidding to a halt. He could feel the hook's weight in his backpack. He scanned his memory, but his brain felt groggy and twitchy at the same time.

"It's our graduation today," John added. "We've gotta head to the auditorium."

"Oh, right!" Barrie said, smacking his forehead. "How could I forget?"

"Yeah, weirdo," Michael said. "Sure you're okay? You've been acting strange lately."

"Yeah, like . . . way spacier than normal," John added. "And that's saying a lot."

Barrie studied his friends' faces. They looked genuinely concerned. He wanted to confide in them and confess everything. Tell them about taking the hook from the museum and making his wish to never grow up, and then how Captain Hook's ghost kept haunting him.

But then he remembered his mother.

She didn't believe him—why would they?

But he was losing his mind. He needed help. He opened his mouth to tell them, but then Michael grabbed his arm and pulled him toward the auditorium.

"Come on, we can't be late for the biggest day of our lives," Michael said.

"Junior high, here we come!" John added with a hoot. "Lost Boys forever!"

They broke out their secret handshake, and for a moment, Barrie forgot about the hook and the pirate's ghost and felt better than he had in days. Maybe Hook's ghost would forget about him and leave him alone. Maybe things would start to get better.

Cheered by that thought, he followed his friends into the auditorium, which was overly chilled by air-conditioning and smelled like a new car. Parents were filing in through the doors, excited to capture their kids traipsing across the stage to receive their certificates.

Barrie scanned the crowd but didn't spot his parents. Michael and John waved to their parents, who had settled into the third row together. They waved, then chatted away like friendly neighbors, mostly because that's exactly what they were.

Strange, Barrie thought. Where were his parents? Not to mention his annoying aunt and cousins. Though he wouldn't mind so much if they missed the ceremony. His parents were probably rushing to get away from their work. They'd been so stressed and busy lately that they were always running late. They'd likely arrive any minute, breathless and scattered but excited to whip out their phones and snap goofy pictures of him parading onstage with his class.

Before he could worry about it further, Mr. Bates rapped on his clipboard and ordered them to settle down. "Line up," he called out. "Alphabetical order, please."

Barrie dutifully assembled with his class backstage, separating from Michael and John and slotting into the proper spot. The ceremony began with their names being called in alphabetical order, one after the next. Each kid walked across the stage to shake the principal's hand, received their certificate, and posed for a picture, then exited the other way.

When Barrie got to the front of the line, his heart

hammered in anticipation. This was his first real graduation. In the fall, he would move up to junior high, and so
much would change. He just hoped that he could stay best
friends with Michael and John. Despite his fears about the
new school, he knew that he could handle it as long as the
Lost Boys stayed together.

He tensed up backstage, waiting for the principal to
call his name.

"Wendy Derry," the principal called out.

Barrie's mouth dropped open.

The principal skipped right over his name to the girl
standing behind him. Wendy shot him a strange look—
like she didn't even know him—then walked past him
onto the stage.

"Hey, Mr. Bates," Barrie said, finding his teacher
backstage. He had a gnawing feeling in his stomach.
"The principal forgot to call my name. What should
I do?"

"What do you mean?" Mr. Bates said, looking
concerned.

"They skipped right to Wendy," Barrie said, certain his teacher would fix it. "There must be some kind

of mistake. The principal didn't call my name to graduate."

Mr. Bates checked his clipboard with the class list on it, then glanced down at Barrie with that glazed-over look.

"Barrie *Darling*?" Mr. Bates said with empty eyes. His voice sounded monotone. "Oh, right. You're still in fifth grade. You'll *always* be in fifth grade, remember?"

"Wh-what do you mean?" Barrie stammered. His stomach sank. "My grades aren't the best, but they're okay. Grady has way worse grades, and they called his name."

"Special kids like you stay kids," Mr. Bates said. "And you stay in my class . . . *forever*."

From backstage, he heard the principal call Michael's name. His best friend marched across the stage and accepted his certificate, pausing to bow for a photo op.

"No, I'm supposed to graduate with my friends," Barrie said, feeling tears spring to his eyes. A lump formed in his throat. "We're all going to junior high together in the fall."

"I'm sorry, but there must be a mistake," Mr. Bates

said. "You can't go to junior high. That's for grown-up kids. You get to stay in fifth grade. I'm your teacher . . . *forever.*"

Barrie started to back away. He couldn't believe what he was hearing or what was happening to him. This was worse than the terrible nightmares and Hook's ghost haunting him. He watched as John crossed the stage, officially graduating.

Still they didn't call Barrie's name. The ceremony wound to a close. His parents never arrived, either, nor did his aunt and cousins. Nobody came to see him. Barrie hid backstage in the shadows by himself, while his classmates cheered and celebrated without him. Michael and John hooted and did their secret handshake, this time without Barrie to share in their ritual.

He felt a tear trickle down his cheek, leaving a trail. He wanted to join his friends, but he felt like a freak who didn't belong.

"This isn't what I meant when I made my wish," he whispered, his voice catching.

But there was nobody there to hear him.

12

YEARBOOKS

School was out for the summer, but when Barrie woke up the next day, he didn't feel his usual excitement at the months of total freedom ahead.

What did any of it mean if he wasn't moving up to junior high with his friends? Not to mention the horrible nightmares. For the last few nights, he had tried to stay up as late as possible, keeping watch for Hook's ghost, but eventually, he always fell into a fitful sleep full of bad dreams. Now that he was awake, he felt even more exhausted than he had before bed. At this rate, he was going to turn into a sleep-deprived zombie like his mother, who needed megadoses of caffeine to function.

Graduation replayed in his head, haunting him just as much as the pirate captain. *You'll always be in fifth grade. . . . I'm your teacher . . . forever.* His teacher's words echoed through his head, hitting him a little bit harder each time. While he had wanted to stay a kid, Barrie hadn't considered what would happen if everyone else grew up, including his best friends.

One of the main reasons that he'd made his wish was to *keep* his best friends—not *lose* them. He remembered them celebrating their graduation without him while he hid backstage. This was all turning out to be the exact opposite of a dream come true.

Even his mom letting him have a second helping of his favorite sugar-bomb cereal didn't cheer him up. In fact, he couldn't believe it, but he was starting to get sick of how sweet it was. It made his teeth hurt and gave him a low-grade headache.

He scowled at the friendly cartoon pirate on the box. "Walk the plank, matey," he whispered.

"Have fun playing all day, kiddo," Mom said, waving him out the door.

"*Fun* . . . what's that?" Rita said, scowling at him from

the kitchen table, where her nose was buried in a thick workbook. High school was out for the school year, but now began something even worse—SAT prep classes.

Whatever that is, Barrie thought, reminding himself that there were still good things about staying a kid. He grabbed his backpack and skateboard. Also, it was still summer break. This was his favorite time of the year because it meant one thing—no school.

His friends wouldn't be moving up to junior high without him for a couple of months. They could still hang at the skate park, try out some new tricks, and look around for some fun trouble to get into. Feeling the tiniest bit better, he mounted his skateboard and headed out.

* * *

He spotted Michael and John lounging with their boards in a shady spot under a big oak tree. Barrie skated up to them. His backpack was strapped to his shoulders with the hook inside.

"Hey, guys! Wassup?" Barrie greeted them.

They both looked up at him, confused.

"Hey, kid," Michael said. "What do you want?"

"Uh, it's summer," Barrie said, kicking his board up and grabbing the end. "We always hang out in the park together."

"*We* hang out?" John said, glancing at Michael. "We don't even know you."

Barrie's mouth dropped open in shock.

"Yeah, do you go to our school?" Michael added. "What're you in, fourth grade?"

"Wh-what?" Barrie stammered.

They just stared up at him. Barrie thought of all the pranks they had played on each other over the years and decided—hoped—that was what was happening now. He forced a laugh.

"Right, nice prank," he said, plopping down next to them.

"What prank?" John said, not laughing or breaking character. "We're serious. What's your name, anyway?"

They both stared at him.

No. No! This is not happening! Barrie thought.

"Guys, I'm Barrie . . . your best friend . . ." he said. "We do *everything* together—"

"Barrie? Barrie . . . We don't know anyone named Barrie," Michael cut him off. "Do we?"

"Nope. And I'm pretty sure we'd remember our *best friend*," John added.

They both snickered at Barrie.

"Nice try, dude," Michael said. "You're just some elementary school loser who wants to hang with the older kids."

"Right, we're in junior high now," John said. "Go play with someone your own age. We've got way more important stuff to do."

Barrie stared at his two best friends in the world, waiting for them to break into grins or tell him that it was just a sick joke. But they remained stone-faced. Being stabbed by a sword couldn't have felt any worse than this.

How could they not remember him?

Feeling heartbroken, Barrie collected his board and sulked away. He could hear them laughing at his expense. "What a weirdo," Michael whispered to John.

"Trying to pretend to be our best friend?" John jeered. "Like how desperate do you have to be?"

This was worse than not being called at graduation.

And missing the concert. And not getting to have a birthday party. Nothing could be worse than this.

Why is this happening to me? Why did I ever make that wish?

Was he really never going to grow up?

As he skated away from the park, he spotted the elementary school in the distance.

There was only one way to be sure.

* * *

Barrie crept around to the side of the school, sticking to the shadows. He ran his hands along the redbrick wall as he went.

It was eerily quiet and deserted now that school was out for the summer. The various summer camps and programs wouldn't start up for another few weeks. He scanned the place for security guards, but even they seemed to have packed up and gone home, as grateful for a break as the kids.

Barrie usually loved the summer. He loved the heat of the sun even when the temperature crested one hundred degrees, which seemed to happen more often every year. He loved the chill of ice cream on his tongue; the long, lazy days spent skateboarding with his friends. *My former friends,* he thought with a shudder, remembering their cold expressions at the park.

Summer would not be the same without them. They were the Lost Boys. But without them, Barrie just felt . . . *lost.*

Still clutching his skateboard, he tried the back entrance by the playground. But it was locked and wouldn't budge. *Too easy,* he thought, releasing the handle.

He crept around to the side of the library, peering through the window. It was dark and empty inside. He could see rows of books spanning back, vanishing into the dark recesses of the spacious room. Clusters of desks with computers and lamps and padded chairs for reading took up the more open areas. The checkout desk was dark and empty.

Glancing around to make sure that nobody was lurking nearby, Barrie pulled the hook out of his backpack. The sharp tip glinted in the midday sunlight. Sweat beaded on his forehead, both from the heat and his nerves.

Then he slid the hook under the window's latch, twisted it, and popped open the lock.

He glanced down at the hook, impressed. Then, he stuffed it back in his backpack and stashed his skateboard in the bushes outside. In one smooth motion, he slid the window open and slithered through it. Being small still had some benefits. This wasn't the first time he'd snuck into a place he didn't belong, and at this rate, it was unlikely to be the last.

The air inside the library smelled stale and felt warmer than normal. Usually, it was kept at subzero temperatures by the blasting air-conditioning. Even so, Barrie felt a chill as he crept around the stacks. He kept expecting a security guard to bust him—or worse—for Captain Hook to appear.

But it was deserted.

After a few moments of searching, he located the right section. His eyes fell on the collection of old-school yearbooks that spanned back decades. The new ones were bright and the pages crisp, while the older ones were yellowed and dusty.

He pulled down the most recent yearbook, flipping

to the page for his fifth-grade class. Colorful pictures of his classmates stared back at him, all familiar faces. Sure enough, his picture was right there along with the other kids in his class. His eyes darted to his friends' portraits.

Michael looked stiff and uncomfortable in his picture. His mom had clearly made him comb his hair into a dorky style and wear that lame polo shirt. Then he found John pulling a goofy face with crossed eyes, even though that wasn't allowed. Leave it to John to always break the rules. Barrie smirked, but then sadness swept through him again.

He remembered their jeering laughter at the park and them telling him to go play with someone his own age.

But I am your age! he had wanted to yell back at them.

The yearbook was proof of that. He'd take it back to the park to show them that he was actually in their class. Maybe it was just an elaborate prank, and they were taking it too far. That had to be it.

Buoyed by that thought, Barrie turned to leave, but then the yearbook from last year caught his eye. It couldn't hurt to bring more than one to prove that they'd been in the same class together since kindergarten. After all, that was how they became best friends in the first place, learning to skateboard after school and falling in love with the same band.

Barrie reached for the yearbook and pulled it down. He flipped to the fourth-grade class pictures, expecting to see his face superimposed in front of the fake blue background staring back at him.

But Barrie didn't see his picture. He double-checked the year and also the alphabetical order. Where was it?

It has to be a mistake.

He located Michael's and John's pictures. They were right where they should be, along with the other kids from his fourth-grade class. But where was Barrie's class picture?

A chill shot through him as he remembered Mr. Bates's words.

You stay in my class . . . forever.

Barrie's fingers trembled as he flipped to fifth grade. Mr. Bates smiled back, and then pictures of his fifth-grade students took up the rest of the page. These faces looked mostly unfamiliar to Barrie. Maybe he'd passed them in the hallways, but they were older than him. Kids mostly stuck with the other kids from their class.

That's when he saw something that made his heart jump. His picture. *Barrie's* picture. Right there in the middle of the fifth-grade class.

This is not happening.

He flipped back to the fourth-grade page, double-checking it. Michael and John hadn't budged. Then he double-checked the year. It all checked out. He should have been in fourth grade, too.

His mouth went dry, and he tasted metal on his tongue. Quickly, he started pulling down yearbooks from the shelf, going back several years. In each yearbook, Barrie was pictured along with the fifth grade. Even when Michael and John were in kindergarten, Barrie was there with the fifth-grade class.

Then, in one book, he spotted . . . *Rita.*

His sister's school picture was right next to his picture in the fifth-grade class.

Barrie Darling. Rita Darling.

Rita looked so young. She looked his age. It was so weird, seeing their two pictures next to one another this way. It made his stomach turn.

We used to be the same age?

Starting to feel panicked, Barrie grabbed the next yearbook. In this one, Rita was back in fourth grade, while Barrie remained in fifth. How could he have ever been *older* than his sister, who was now sixteen years old and in high school?

He grabbed more yearbooks. Year after year, Barrie stayed in fifth grade while his classmates changed and strangers surrounded him. He found one where his sister was in kindergarten. Her girlish smile and gap-toothed grin sent a shudder down Barrie's spine.

Chilled, he dropped the yearbook. They had piled up at his feet in a big jumble. Hundreds of kids grinned back at him, looking ghostly in the dim lighting. Most of them were strangers to his eyes.

With trembling hands, he reached for a yearbook that was labeled CLASS OF 1984. That was decades ago. He located the page for the fifth-grade class. Mr.

Bates hadn't been the teacher back then. A strange woman with permed hair and thick glasses grinned back. He glanced down at the pictures, then gasped in shock.

"No, it can't be true," he whispered.

But sure enough, there was his class picture, surrounded by strange, old-timey kids.

I wasn't even alive in 1984.

But he was in the school yearbook, the same exact age as he was right now. He slammed the yearbook shut in horror. It tumbled from his hands, hitting the carpeted floor with a thud.

Suddenly, the pages started flipping on their own, turning faster and faster. They landed back on Barrie's class portrait from 1984. He was wearing strange clothes—acid-washed jeans and a baggy, fluorescent yellow sweatshirt. His hair was trimmed into a severe bowl cut.

His own face stared back at him from the pages, even though it was impossible.

Suddenly, a dark shadow fell over him.

SECOND STAR TO THE FRIGHT

It was accompanied by a deep, jeering laugh that made Barrie's skin crawl.

Just as Barrie began to cautiously turn around, a sword slashed out of the shadows, shredding the 1984 class yearbook and scratching Barrie's face from existence.

13

ALL HANDS
ON DECK

Barrie bolted from the library in a panic. He abandoned the yearbooks, not bothering to bring the evidence that he'd come to collect. He ran down the row, but Hook's ghost chased after him.

Thump. Thump.

Hook's dark shadow grew closer. The footsteps grew louder.

Barrie tried to turn on the speed. He had to get out of the library and get someplace where there were people. Someone who could help him. Then he heard something else—metal scraping against metal. Hook had unsheathed his sword.

"Scurvy brat, I shall have my revenge!" the pirate's voice boomed through the stacks.

He slashed at Barrie's head.

Barrie dodged the sword, darting around the corner to the next aisle. He ran faster, weaving through the stacks. He sprinted for the window. He could see the bright sunlight shining through it. He was almost there. Just one more turn. He bolted down the next row.

But Hook's ghost stepped out right in front of him, blocking the escape route. The pirate captain was lit from the back so that only his dark silhouette was visible. Hook raised his shadowy sword. His voice reverberated through the library.

"Blasted kid, I'll make ye walk the plank!"

Barrie staggered backward, then turned and ran back the way he'd come. He hooked a right, but this row dead-ended at a wall. He was trapped between the tall bookcases. He whipped around in a blind panic.

This time, there was no escape. Nowhere to run. Nowhere to hide.

Thump. Thump.

Hook's ghost advanced on him with his sword raised.

For a split second, the sunlight caught on the pirate's other arm—which ended in a bloody stump. Of course, Barrie had taken his hook. He felt a surge of guilt. No wonder Captain Hook's ghost wanted revenge on him.

Thump. Thump.

Hook's ghost drew closer, rising over him like a dark shadow.

Barrie felt his mouth go dry, as adrenaline surged through him. The air felt suddenly colder. He shuddered violently, backing away. Desperately, he scanned for a way out.

Thump. Thump.

Barrie clawed open his backpack, searching for the hook. Maybe if he gave it back, then the ghost would stop haunting him. His fingers seized on the rusty metal.

"Look, Mr. Pirate . . . Captain . . . sir . . ." Barrie stammered, holding up the hook. "I made a big mistake . . . I shouldn't have taken it . . . you can have it back. . . ."

Still, Hook's ghost advanced on him. Barrie backed up even more, his back hitting the wall with a thump.

"Please," Barrie begged. "Please . . ."

That's when he heard another noise coming from above him.

Tick-tock. Tick-tock.

It was soft but clearly audible. Barrie glanced up at the wall. He was standing under a wall clock, the old-fashioned kind with hands that ticked around the numbers on the face.

Tick-tock. Tick-tock.

He braced himself for Hook's ghost to strike him down with his sword.

But when he looked back, the pirate was gone.

* * *

Barrie scrambled through the library window and tumbled out, landing flat in the bushes next to his skateboard with a loud thud. It knocked the wind out of him.

Bright sunlight glared down, momentarily blinding him. He struggled to catch his breath and blinked to clear his vision, then skated away from the school in a panic. He didn't know why Hook's ghost had vanished back there. The last thing he remembered was backing up against the wall under that clock. Then when he turned back, the pirate was gone.

But he didn't plan to stick around to find out if Hook was coming back.

As he skated away from the school cutting back toward his cul-de-sac, the horror of what he'd found in the library rushed through him—the school pictures of him as a fifth grader, year after year after year. When he'd made his wish to stay a kid forever, that wasn't what he'd meant.

Even worse, Hook's ghost was still after him and wanted revenge. Clearly, he was growing more impatient, too. This time, Hook came after him in broad daylight in a public place. That meant that Barrie didn't have much time left. It kept getting worse.

He had to find a way to make it stop. He had to reverse his wish.

But how was he going to do that?

He felt completely alone and lost. Usually, whenever he had a problem, he would talk to Michael and John. They were the Lost Boys. They always helped him, no matter what. Even in his books, the brothers solved mysteries together. They each had different skills and abilities. They needed each other to solve the cases. They couldn't do it alone.

That's when Barrie realized—*I need my friends to help me.*

Even if they don't remember me.

Barrie cut back through the skate park, but his friends were gone. He hopped on his skateboard, heading for their cul-de-sac. He rode up to Michael's two-story redbrick house, then slipped around back through the backyard, peering through his bedroom window.

Just as expected, Michael and John were hunched on the bed playing a video game, having sought refuge from the afternoon heat in the air-conditioning. Their skate-boards lay abandoned by the door, along with their Vans. Candy wrappers littered the bedspread. Usually, Barrie would be there with them, and he felt a sharp pang over being left out.

I'm going to fix this, he thought. *I just need to convince them to help.*

With a deep breath, Barrie reached out and rapped on the door. *Tat-tat-tat-tat-a-tat.* He used their "secret code."

Michael and John both startled. They paused the game and padded over to the window. Their eyes landed on Barrie. They didn't look happy to see him.

"It's that weird kid from the park," John whispered. Michael slid the window partway open.

"How do you know the *secret* Lost Boys code?" Michael demanded.

"Yeah, have you been spying on us?" John added, his eyes narrowed.

Barrie took a deep breath.

"I know the code because I'm your best friend," he said firmly. "I'm one of the Lost Boys, too. The code was my idea. I helped invent it."

"What do you mean?" Michael said, glancing uneasily at John.

"Oh, please. Don't start listening to him," John scoffed. Then he scowled at Barrie. "Nice try, dude. But we don't even know you—"

"Yeah, but you *did* know me," Barrie said, plowing forward. "We used to do everything together! Only I made a terrible mistake. That's why I'm here. I need your help. I don't know where else to turn. You're my only chance."

"Come on, shut the window," John said, rolling his eyes. "I wanna beat my high score."

But Michael hesitated. His eyes darted to Barrie. "But he did know the code."

"Yeah—and it's not all I know," Barrie said, seizing on the opening. "Remember how in kindergarten, you lost your first tooth during recess on the very first day of school? And I helped you find it?"

"That could've happened to anyone," Michael said. "Just a good guess—"

"It was under the monkey bars," Barrie went on, searching his memory for every detail. "We'd been playing chicken, trying to knock each other off. And when you fell, it popped right out of your mouth."

John snickered. "He's right. That was classic. I can't believe we found it."

"Yeah, but it was just us," Michael said, nodding to John. "You weren't there."

"But I *was* there," Barrie insisted. "You just don't remember me. The tooth fairy brought you a whole ten bucks for your tooth. It was like a tooth fairy record. We spent it all on candy and comics. We were on a sugar-and-superhero high like all week."

"Wait, how'd you know about that?" Michael said.

"Because I told you already . . . *I'm your best friend*," Barrie said. Before they could doubt him, he recounted other memories from their years of friendship—secrets and details about their lives—things that only the Lost Boys knew.

John started to look afraid. "But how . . . is this possible? I've never even seen you before today."

"Yeah, how can you know all of that?" Michael went on with a frown.

"Secret handshake?" Barrie said, reaching his hand out.

He knew this would seal the deal.

They hesitated, but then John shrugged, and Barrie's heart leaped. They executed their secret handshake to perfection. "Lost Boys forever!" they chanted together. As Barrie slid his hands from Michael's and John's grips, he could tell that he'd won them over.

For now.

They all grinned, and if felt like old times. But then they fell more serious.

"But why don't we remember you?" John said. "If you're our best friend?"

Barrie unzipped his backpack and showed them the hook. It glinted in the fading daylight. "Because I stole this from the pirate ship at the maritime museum and made a wish to never grow up, and it worked . . . only it was a huge mistake."

"Whoa," John said, his eyes wide as he checked out the hook. "Pirate magic?"

"You didn't want to grow up?" Michael asked.

"Well, I thought staying a kid sounded great—until it actually happened," Barrie said. "Now everybody is growing up without me, and I'm stuck as a kid forever."

"What do you mean?" Michael said. "Is that why we can't remember you?"

Barrie nodded. "That's what I think. Let me in, and I'll explain everything. I have to find a way to make it stop."

Michael hesitated. John looked worried. For a second, Barrie thought he'd lost them. He knew how crazy it all sounded, and he hadn't even told them about Captain Hook's ghost haunting him and wanting revenge.

But then Michael slid the window open and gestured for Barrie to climb in.

"Lost Boys don't forget their friends," Michael said in a firm voice. "If we can find a way to help you, then we'll do it."

"Yeah, if anyone can fix it," John chimed in, "it's the Lost Boys, right?"

As Barrie climbed through the window and joined his friends inside, one thought shot through his head: *I just hope it's true.*

14

CAPTAIN JAMES HOOK

"It's a long story," Barrie said, settling onto Michael's outer space comforter. Everything in this bedroom felt as familiar as his own house because he'd practically grown up here.

The paused video game flickered on the screen and lit up the room as the sun began its lazy summer descent outside, painting the sky bright pink.

John furrowed his brow. "Just start at the beginning," he said slowly. "And don't leave anything out. You never know when some detail ends up being important."

"Okay, it all started right before my birthday," Barrie said. "When my family took me to the maritime museum."

"Your birthday?" Michael said.

"Yeah, the one you both forgot," Barrie said, feeling a fresh wave of sadness. "But I'll get to that part later."

Then, before they could interrupt him again, Barrie told his friends everything, trying not to leave out any details. He told them about the trip to the museum and the boring tour of the pirate ship. How he'd thought it was like his mystery books, and he'd snuck off and discovered the secret compartment with the hook and letter.

He told them about making his wish to never grow up and how it seemed great at first, even though everyone forgot about his birthday. But then his wish backfired horribly. He even told them about the yearbooks, and how he always stayed in fifth grade.

"Ugh, that does sound horrible!" John said. "Having Mr. Bates for eternity?"

"Yeah, one school year was bad enough," Michael agreed with a shudder. "But staying in his class forever?"

"Yeah, I thought staying a kid forever would be great—but it's a curse," Barrie said. "I didn't graduate. My best friends have forgotten me. And who knows what will happen next if I don't stop it?"

Michael picked the rusty hook up off the bed. He ran

his fingers over it, wincing when he touched the razor-sharp tip.

"So, you're saying that this hook belonged to . . . Captain Hook," Michael said. "Like *the* Captain James Hook."

"Yes, I found it in his captain's cabin," Barrie said with a nod. "And the letter is signed by him . . ." he added, running his fingertip over the signature line on the parchment letter.

Michael cracked open his laptop and tapped on the keys, bringing up a portrait of Captain Hook. It was the same one displayed in the *Jolly Roger*. A fresh rush of fear crashed through Barrie's chest at the sight of it. Hook's beady eyes bore into him as if accusing him.

Bloody thief, I'll have my revenge!

"That's who it belonged to?" John said, flinching back from the screen. "Dude, bad life choice stealing from a scary pirate captain."

Hook's visage was terrifying even when rendered in a painting.

"Yeah, it says here that he was one of the most blood-thirsty pirates in history," Michael said, reading off the website. "His exploits on the high seas were legendary."

"Yup, I'm sure it's him," Barrie said, his voice wavering. He took a deep breath, knowing the next part was going to sound truly insane. "The thing is . . . he's been haunting me."

Michael looked up in surprise. "Like a ghost?"

"Yes, that's what I think," Barrie said. "I mean, he must have died a long time ago. His pirate ship is in a *history* museum. But I know I'm not imagining it. He's really after me."

"But ghosts aren't real," Michael said, biting his lower lip. "Plus, you said he can, like, affect things in the real world. He scratched your floor. He left that message on your door."

"Yeah, that's not very ghostly," John agreed. "Sounds like a real pirate dude."

Barrie shook his head. "But he's hundreds of years old. There's no way he could still be alive . . . he has to be a ghost. That's the only possible explanation for what's happening."

"Unless . . ." Michael said, reaching for the parchment letter.

"Unless . . . what?" Barrie said, studying his friend's

face. He knew how Michael got when he'd hit upon a brilliant idea. He turned all quiet and pensive, just like right now.

Michael looked up from the letter. "Unless . . . he is still *alive*."

"Wait, what do you mean?" Barrie said with a start. "That's impossible."

"Look here," Michael said, pointing to the letter's cursive script. "This letter you found says that the hook grants whoever possesses it the power to *never grow up*."

"That's right," Barrie said. "And it works, too."

Michael nodded. "Right, so what if it did the same thing to Captain Hook?"

"You mean, it made it so he stopped aging?" John said, catching on. "Interesting theory, Sherlock. That would explain how he could still be alive after all this time."

"Yeah, and it would also explain why he's so angry that Barrie stole his hook," Michael went on. "I mean, aside from the poor aesthetics of walking around with a bloody stump."

John snorted a laugh. "Not sure a hook is exactly fashionable."

"Uh, it is if you're a freaky pirate captain," Michael said. "It's practically required. Anyway, if Captain Hook doesn't get that hook back, then he could grow old and die."

"And soon," John added. "That's probably why he's growing more impatient and attacking Barrie in public in the middle of the day. I bet his life is literally ticking away."

"So, you think if I give the hook back," Barrie said, processing it all and tapping the letter, "then Captain Hook will leave me alone—and it will also reverse the curse?"

Michael nodded. "Yeah, I think you have only one choice—you have to return the hook to Captain Hook's ship. And you have to do it tonight. You can't wait much longer. Not only is Hook growing bolder, but the curse also seems to be growing stronger, too."

"Right, you don't have much time left," John added. "Who knows what could happen next? You could wake up tomorrow and your parents wouldn't even remember you."

"Yeah, and Rita," Barrie said. They looked at him blankly. "My evil sister," he reminded them. "Though, that might not be the *worst* thing."

They all cracked up. Barrie's eyes flicked over the letter and rusty hook, then back to his friends. Captain Hook seemed to stare at them from the laptop. Barrie shuddered.

"Think it'll work?" he said, feeling the first flicker of hope in a long time.

"Well, what other choice do you have?" John pointed out.

"Yeah, exactly," Michael agreed. His eyes darted to the hook lying on the bedspread. "The power to not grow up will leave you, just like it left Hook when you stole it."

"You're right," Barrie said. "Also, if I give Hook what he wants, then hopefully he'll leave me alone."

Barrie stared at his friends in gratitude. He'd known he needed their help. He just couldn't believe that he had waited so long to trust them with his problems. Despite all the terrible things that had happened to him since he stole the hook, Barrie felt almost *normal* sitting with his best friends, trying to solve a problem. This was what friends were for, right?

Not just the good times, but also the bad ones.

"Okay, that means I have to sneak back onto the *Jolly*

Roger somehow," Barrie said, thinking aloud. "I'll have to get past the guards. It'll be dangerous. If I get caught, then I could be in big trouble. I mean, I stole an artifact from a museum—"

"Don't you mean . . . *we*?" Michael cut him off. "*We* could get in a lot of trouble."

"Uh, yeah," John added. "We're not letting you go alone."

"No way," Barrie said, shaking his head. "It's way too dangerous. Didn't you hear what I said? I could get arrested. Not to mention Captain Hook is after me. I'd hate it if you got into trouble because of my bad decisions. Or worse . . ." He trailed off, feeling a stab of guilt.

But then Michael grinned and thrust his hand in the air.

"Aye, matey, sounds like an adventure," he said in a cockney accent. "I'm in!"

"Lost Boys forever," John added. But then he frowned. "But how are we going to get there? The maritime museum is all the way out at the marina. We don't have much time left."

"Yeah, we can't exactly skate there," Michael said. "It would take forever."

Barrie frowned, racking his brain. He stared at the hook, remembering that one moment on the pirate ship—the moment he and his sister had bonded.

"Right, I've got an idea," Barrie said in a determined voice. "Let's meet in front of my house in an hour." Michael and John shared a look.

"Ummm . . . where's that?"

* * *

Barrie rode his skateboard home. His Vans scuffed the pavement, propelling him ahead. The sun was slipping below the horizon, casting his quaint cul-de-sac in shadows. All he heard was the faint call of the cicadas' summer-song and the familiar sound of his skateboard wheels.

But then, something else.

Thump. Thump.

Heavy footsteps. Coming from the shadows.

Hook was coming for him.

Feeling a jolt of adrenaline, Barrie tensed up and skated faster. He sped across the cul-de-sac. The shadows cast by the fading sunlight seemed to stretch as if to grab him, but then their dark tendrils passed over him harmlessly. He strained his ears for those heavy footsteps.

A few minutes later—but what felt like an eternity— he pulled up in front of his house, then kicked up his board, snagging it by the end. His backpack hung on his shoulders. The hook was nestled inside, as always.

He hurried up to the front door, but then he reeled back in shock. A dagger stuck out of the wood panel in the center of the door, spearing an old piece of parchment paper.

His eyes scanned the letter. It was printed with jagged cursive.

Return my hook—or your family will perish!

Barrie tore the parchment down, his hands shaking. The dagger remained stuck in the front door. It looked ancient, like something that would've belonged to a pirate.

Barrie stared at the jagged cursive. He knew one thing with certainty.

It wasn't just about him anymore. Now his family was in danger, too.

He didn't have much time left.

15

TICKET TO RIDE

"**N**o way, Goober," Rita said, not even looking up from her SAT prep workbook. "Carpool is torture enough."

"Pretty please?" Barrie begged. "With a cherry on top? Just this one time. I need your help. I need a lift out to the marina to meet my friends."

He wrung his hands. He'd stuffed the parchment letter in his pocket, but the words were seared into his brain.

"It's late," Rita said with a sigh. "Mom and Dad are working late. That means I'm in charge, and I'm not budging. I gotta finish this stupid exercise."

"But I really need a ride," Barrie said, trying to think

fast. "I'll make it up to you. I wouldn't ask if it wasn't important."

Finally, she lifted her head. She frowned when she actually saw him.

"What's got you so jumpy? You look like you've just seen a ghost."

"Uh, I just really need a ride," he said. "Come on, please just help me out."

He couldn't tell her about Captain Hook. There was no way that she'd believe him. He remembered his mom's reaction at the museum. Rita would be worse.

"Why do you wanna go out to the marina so bad anyway?" she asked, giving him a suspicious look. "I don't buy it. My sibling radar is on high alert. What aren't you telling me? Spit it out already."

Her eyes bore into him. Sibling radar was no joke. His sister could be super psychic when she wanted to be.

"Fine, there's this cute girl," Barrie said, his cheeks burning. "And she texted me that she'll be hanging out by the marina with her friends today."

Rita giggled. "Ah, talking to girls. No wonder you

look like you've seen a ghost. That's, like, the scariest thing ever, right?'

"Don't rub it in," Barrie mumbled, even though it was a lie. Just the concept of discussing girls with his sister freaked him out almost as bad as Captain Hook did. And it was certainly far more embarrassing.

"Wow, it's almost worth giving you a ride just to watch you squirm," Rita said. "Does this girl have an actual name?"

Barrie glared at his sister. "No way, I'm not telling you. You'll never let me live it down. I know how you operate."

Rita stared right back at him. She fingered her car keys sitting on the kitchen table. "Then you're not getting a ride."

"Fine. Her name is Wendy," Barrie muttered. "And that's all the details I'm giving you."

"Oh, Barrie's got a crush on . . . W-E-N-D-Y," Rita said, making a kissy face. "I can't wait to tell Brooke about this. She's gonna die laughing."

On second thought, maybe he should skate out there.

Nothing was worth this. Giving his sister leverage over him was a terrible idea.

"Do that—and you'll pay," Barrie said, regretting asking for help.

"Goober, you're not exactly in a position to bargain," Rita said, firing off a quick text to Brooke. "As I recall, you're just a kid, and I'm the one with the driver's license."

"Ugh, I hate you," Barrie muttered. But she was right. She had him cornered. Just the way she liked it.

"I *love* you, too," Rita said, scooping up her keys. "I'll give you a ride, but just 'cause I'm feeling generous tonight. And I hate that stupid prep class. But this is a onetime deal—don't make a habit of it."

* * *

"Dude, your sister is driving way over the speed limit," John said nervously as Rita sped off, leaving them down the street from the entrance to the marina. She'd promised to pick them up in two hours sharp. "And what's this about you having a crush on Wendy?"

"Wait, Wendy Derry?" Michael said. "Uh, she's kinda weird."

Barrie sighed. "No, I made all that up so Rita would give us a ride. I was trying to think of something fast . . . and well . . . that's the first idea that popped into my head."

"*Wendy* was the first idea?" Michael said, looking at John with a sly smile. "Uh-oh, ya know what that means?"

"Wait, what're you talking about?" Barrie said. "It's not true—I swear it! I just made that up to convince Rita."

"Dude, it means that you actually like her," Michael said. "Like, if you're stressed out—and she's your first thought?"

"Yeah, you wanna kiss Wendy," John said, making a puckered face. "Like, if the zombie apocalypse hit, her face would flash before your eyes. That's how you *know* it's true love."

"For the record, I don't like Wendy—or any other lame girls from our class," Barrie said with a dramatic sigh. "She probably doesn't even remember me!"

"See, you do like her!" Michael said triumphantly. "Or else why would you care if she forgot about you?"

Barrie stormed ahead in a funk. This was the *last* thing

he wanted to think about. He had far more important things to think about. But then doubt crept into his mind.

Why *had* he thought up that story for Rita?

He shook his head, clearing the thought. He didn't like girls. They talked too much. They giggled at things that weren't even funny. They smelled like hair spray and baby powder. Basically, they made zero sense. His sister proved that. And they were scary, too.

"Look, we have more important things to worry about," Barrie said, skidding to a halt on the sidewalk next to the guardrail that looked over the water. The waves churned and sloshed up against the rocks down below, spritzing his face. "Like how do I get on that pirate ship?"

Barrie pointed across the marina to the *Jolly Roger*, which was docked in its usual spot by the gates to the maritime museum. It was late and already closed. There was a main building that housed the museum, but the pirate ship had its own entrance over by the water.

"Let's go check it out," John suggested, pointing to the ship.

Together they jogged over and hid near the ticket booth. If you bought a ticket to the museum, it granted you access to both the main museum and the pirate ship. The gate that led to the *Jolly Roger*'s gangplank was chained shut. The ship was dark since it was after hours. The skull and crossbones flag flapped in the stiff breeze whipping off the ocean.

Barrie swallowed hard. The gangplank swayed and buckled as the waves churned under it. He was still afraid of the ocean and whatever lurked under those dark waves.

"So, how do we get onto the ship?" he asked, feeling his stomach twist.

He scanned for the security guards, spotting one ambling down the sidewalk in front of the main museum building. His gut jutted over his belt. He didn't look very formidable. But he could always summon help. And the *Jolly Roger* was right in his line of sight.

"Right, I count just the one guard over there," Michael said, following Barrie's gaze toward the security guard by the main museum. "I bet it's just that one rent-a-cop."

"Yup, and that lock on the gate," John said, pointing to the hefty padlock. The metal gate to their right blocked the entrance to the gangplank that led to the *Jolly Roger*.

"How do I get past the gate and onto the ship?" Barrie

said, following the guard's movement back and forth in front of the museum. "Without him noticing?"

The guard was positioned where he was sure to notice anything awry by the marina. From his vantage point, he could keep an eye on both the main museum and the ship.

"Okay, it's just like that time we snuck into the skate park after dark, remember?" Michael said. "We'll distract the security guard, then you can jump over the gate."

"Oh right, the old 'our parents forgot to pick us up; we're helpless lost kids' routine?" Barrie said, remembering how it always worked like a charm on security guards. They wanted nothing more than to prove they were useful. They loved helping lost kids.

Barrie smiled at his friends. All three had slipped back into their Lost Boys mode. This wasn't the first time they'd snuck into a place where they didn't belong.

"Yup, it's genius," John said. "Don't tell me—you invented it?"

"Yup, sure did," Barrie said. "It was my idea the first time we tried it."

"Jeez, I still don't remember you," Michael said. "But I sure missed you."

"Yeah, glad you're back," John said. "When you notice the guard is distracted, vault the gate. Just move fast. Not sure how long we can keep his attention away from the ship."

"But only if you tell us first . . ." Michael added with a wicked grin. "How badly do you want to kiss Wendy Derry?"

"Shut up," Barrie said, smiling in spite of himself. "I don't like her."

They all laughed.

Barrie waited while his friends approached the guard. He could see John even working up some fake tears to sell their "lost boys" story. He watched while concern spread over the guard's face. He turned his back away from the pirate ship. This was his chance.

As soon as the security guard turned away from the marina, escorting Michael and John toward the main museum building's entrance, presumably to help them contact their parents, Barrie leaped out of his hiding spot. Of course, Michael and John wouldn't give him their real names or phone numbers. Eventually, the guard would catch on—and be very unhappy.

SECOND STAR TO THE FRIGHT

But it should buy Barrie enough time to get onto the ship. He sped up to the gate, then clambered up the metal bars before flipping over the top and landing in a crouch. All those days perfecting tricks at the skate park were good for something. Not to mention all that time spent sleuthing around like the kid detectives in his mystery books, pretending to solve cases.

Barrie glanced back toward the main museum. The guard was still occupied with Michael and John. He'd pulled out his phone to call for help. But Barrie had to hurry; as soon as their parents didn't pick up the phone, the guard would catch on to their prank. And Barrie would get busted.

He bolted away from the gate and down the gangplank. It swayed under his feet. Suddenly, his sneakers slipped on the wet wood. He plunged toward the side. He grabbed onto the rope railing. It seared his palms. His face was only inches from the water.

Tick-tock. Tick-tock.

That strange noise echoed up from the water.

All of a sudden, a dark shape darted past. It had a long, spiny tail.

16

AHOY, MATEY!

Barrie tried to scramble back from the water, but his feet slipped again, almost sending him overboard. The wood was too slick. His heart hammered. He was terrified of the ocean.

Tick-tock. Tick-tock.

The shadow was still circling under the gangplank.

Finally, Barrie yanked himself back to his feet, using the rope railing. *That was close.* He still didn't know what was lurking in the water—and he didn't want to know.

One thought shot through his head.

If I get through this, then I'm spending the rest of my life on dry land.

With his heart pounding in his chest, Barrie sprinted

the rest of the way down the gangplank, stowing away aboard the pirate ship. His feet pounded against the slick wooden deck.

Overhead, the masts loomed like wooden spikes, while the skull and crossbones on the black flag stared down at him. He passed the plank that jutted out over the ocean. Just looking at it gave him chills. The ocean seemed hungry beneath it.

He could hear Captain Hook's voice in this head.

I'll make ye walk the plank!

He glanced around nervously, scanning the shadows for the pirate. So far, the ship appeared deserted. All he had to do was sneak back down into the captain's cabin—and put the hook back where he found it in the secret compartment. Then, all of this would stop.

It has to stop.

He gripped his backpack straps in determination, feeling the hook's weight inside. He'd known it was wrong to steal it, but he'd done it anyway. He couldn't believe how foolish he had been to think that never growing up sounded like a good idea.

Of course, all the sugary treats and extra television

time had been great at first. Not to mention getting out of his chores and homework. But the excitement had worn off fast and things had turned sour. This was the only way that he could keep his friends and make Captain Hook stop.

I'll fix it, he thought as he raced down the deck. *Even if it's the last thing I do.*

He had almost reached the stairs that lead down to the captain's cabin. Relief rushed through him, but then he heard something that made him skid to a halt.

Thump. Thump.

Barrie glanced back. A tall, dark figure stepped out onto the deck. His beady eyes bored into Barrie. The rest of his face was dark—cast into shadow—but there was no mistaking who it was.

His voice thundered out.

"Blasted idiot, how dare you sneak onto my ship!"

Captain Hook unsheathed his sword. His other hand ended in a stump, where the hook should have been. He slashed at Barrie. The sharp metal whizzed by his head as he dodged it.

"Mr. Pirate . . . I mean, Captain Hook . . . sir . . ." Barrie stammered, backing away with his hands raised. But Captain Hook lurched at him, slashing at Barrie with the sword.

Whoosh.

Barrie ducked away, backing up more. "Look, I brought your hook back! Just please, make this stop. It was wrong to take it. I want to grow up after all—"

"Bloody thief and liar!" Captain Hook said.

"But I'll give your hook back," Barrie said, backing away. "I never should've taken it. And then I'll leave your ship for good. I'm really, really sorry—"

"Think you can make a fool of Hook?" Captain Hook snarled at him. "You're not the first boy to play a prank on me—but you will be the last. I want my revenge!"

Clearly, the pirate doesn't want to be reasonable, Barrie thought.

With that, he turned and ran as fast as he could toward the stairs that lead down to the interior deck. Maybe if he put the hook back in his cabin, then it would break the curse and the pirate would stop attacking him. The hook was what the pirate wanted, right?

Barrie sprinted down the steps. He took them two at

a time, almost tripping and falling flat on his face. Behind him, he could hear Captain Hook's heavy boots pounding the deck—*thump, thump*—and his sword swooshing through the air.

Captain Hook was getting closer.

Barrie hit the bottom of the stairs, right as the ship rocked under his feet. Through the windows in the side, he could see that a big storm was sweeping into the bay. The winds had picked up dramatically, driving the waves and making them churn.

Lightning pulsed in the sky, lighting up the ocean and making it look wild and dangerous. The ship swayed more, lurching dramatically sideways.

Barrie had to struggle to stay upright, grabbing on to the wall. His eyes locked on the door at the end of the hall. He could just make out the outline in the dim light.

"Scurvy brat, I'll have my revenge!" Captain Hook yelled down the stairs.

Barrie darted down the hall, past the painting of Hook, and reached the door to the captain's cabin. He could still hear Captain Hook's voice chasing after him.

"I'm not leavin' this harbor until I get my revenge," the pirate yelled. "You can't make a fool of Hook!"

The sign on the door still read CLOSED FOR REST-ORATION. But Barrie didn't care. He wrestled with the bronze doorknob, desperate to get away from Captain Hook.

But it didn't budge—the door was locked.

Just then, the ship rocked violently as another wave hit it. Barrie fell to his knees. Panicked, he tried to stand up.

Thump. Thump.

His eyes fell on a pair of black boots as they stepped into view.

Barrie looked up to see Captain Hook's shadowy figure stretch over him. He raised his sword overhead, then brought it down.

"Caught you, scurvy brat!"

Then everything went black.

17

WALK THE PLANK

Barrie woke up with a start—and he was surprised to still be alive.

Where am I? he thought in a daze.

It took a minute for him to recognize his surroundings and for everything to come back to him. The last thing he remembered was Captain Hook's sword swinging down at him.

Then blackness.

The pirate must have knocked him unconscious with the blunt end of that sword. That was the only reason Barrie was still alive. The room was dark, but outside the ship, the storm continued to rage. Bolts of lightning pulsed, lighting up the room at uneven intervals.

When the next one hit, he scanned the area. He was in the captain's cabin, sitting in a tall-backed wooden chair.

In the next flash of lightning, he spotted the rusty hook. It lay on the desk in front of him, nestled back in the velvet-lined box. It rested on top of an old maritime map that depicted an unfamiliar world, marked with strange locations.

Mermaid Lagoon. Skull Rock. Hangman's Tree.

Barrie scanned the map, but none of the places looked familiar. Then the cabin fell dark again. He tried to get up—but his arms wouldn't move. He looked down. He was bound to the chair by scratchy, thick rope. He struggled against it, but the ropes held him in place.

Suddenly, the ship swayed and rocked on the waves. His eyes darted to the window. Fear surged through him. They'd set sail, heading for the open ocean. He could still make out the marina behind them, but it was growing smaller.

Panic seized Barrie's heart. Not only were his chances of escaping getting dimmer with each passing second, but he was also deathly afraid of the ocean. It had been his greatest fear for as long as he could remember, ever since Rita had made him watch that stupid old killer shark movie when he was a little kid.

"No, let me go!" Barrie yelled, struggling against the ropes, even though it was hopeless. They wouldn't budge.

That's when he heard footsteps behind him. *Thump. Thump.*

He tried to look back, but he couldn't turn his head enough. The rope held him fast. The next pulse of lightning lit up the cabin—casting a long shadow over him.

Captain Hook.

The pirate paced in the shadows. His heavy footfalls echoed in the cabin.

"Wh-where are you taking me?" Barrie stammered. "Please, let me go—"

The violent rocking of the ship in the storm cut him off, making his stomach lurch. Bile flooded his throat, singeing it and making his mouth taste sour.

He jerked his gaze to the window. They were moving fast, but the marina was still visible. That meant he still had a chance to escape. But the further away they got, the less likely it was that he could make it back. Had Michael and John seen the ship set sail? Had the guard? Maybe someone was coming after him.

"We're going to a *special* place with a *special* name," Captain Hook said, still pacing in the shadows. Suddenly, a dagger arced down, stabbing the map and impaling the desk. Barrie jerked his head back.

The dagger had speared two words—*Never Land*. It looked like the dagger that had been jammed into his front door.

"Wh-what's that . . . place?" Barrie choked out.

Nothing about it looked friendly. Even the names of the places looked ominous.

"Oh, it's for lost boys like you who don't want to grow up," Captain Hook snarled. "Just follow the second star to the right and straight on till morning."

"But I have to go home!" Barrie pleaded. He wriggled his hands, trying to escape. One of his wrists slipped free from the ropes. "My parents will miss me. Even my sister. They'll look for me—"

"Silly boy, soon enough they'll forget all about you," Hook said. "You're the one who didn't want to grow up, remember? When we get there, you can walk the plank. Let it be a lesson to all the scurvy brats not to mess with Captain Hook."

"But sir, you got what you wanted—I brought the hook back," Barrie said, feeling tears prick his eyes. "You can let me go. I swear, I won't tell anyone you kidnapped me. You can get away—"

"What I wanted, blithering idiot, was revenge!" Captain Hook yelled.

"Wait, that's right," Barrie said, thinking fast. "You said I wasn't the first kid to play a childish prank on you. Who was the other kid? Did he get away?"

"Oh, I'll still find him and make him pay," Captain Hook ranted. "Thinks he can play a prank on Captain Hook?"

While he continued ranting about the kid who'd gotten away, Barrie wriggled his wrist, getting it free from the ropes. Then he reached for the hook, snagging it from the desk. He used it to saw at the ropes at his ankles, cutting himself free from the chair.

The ropes hit the floor with a thud, drawing the pirate's attention.

"Come back, thief!" Captain Hook screamed. But Barrie didn't wait.

He leaped up and darted for the door. His sweaty hands slipped on the doorknob. A dagger whipped by his head, hitting the door by his ear.

Thunk.

But he finally got the doorknob to twist. The heavy door squeaked open. He bolted through it, slamming it shut behind him. He heard the pirate's heavy body slam into the door as the ship rocked dramatically, throwing them around.

Barrie staggered back to his feet and ran for the stairs. He bolted to the upper deck. The turbulent skies had started spitting rain. It hit the ship and stung his face. The white sails were unfurled, whipping in the strong winds.

His eyes fixed on the marina in the distance, fading away behind them. The ship was moving fast. He didn't have much time before they left the safety of the bay. Out in the storm, the open ocean would be far more dangerous.

Barrie ran down the ship's deck, looking for a life raft

or escape boat—or anything that could help him get to safety. He was running past the plank when suddenly something snagged his neck, jerking him back.

"Got you, blasted kid!" Captain Hook hissed in his ear. He held Barrie by the neck. His grip was iron-tight.

Barrie was trapped. There was no way to escape now. Then, suddenly, that dark shadow swam past the ship, cutting through the water and circling by them.

Tick-tock. Tick-tock.

The ticking noise echoed out of the waves.

That was when the strangest thing happened— Captain Hook released his grip on Barrie's neck. The dark shadow in the water made another pass by the ship.

Tick-tock. Tick-tock.

The pirate cowered back from the water. "No, he wants the rest of me!" Captain Hook whined, sounding petrified. "Get him away from me! Help me, I'll do anything!"

Barrie felt confused, then it dawned on him. He remembered how Hook had vanished from the library when he heard the ticking of the clock on the wall. He was terrified of that sound.

And probably for good reason.

Tick-tock. Tick-tock.

Barrie fixed his eyes on the water, where the dark shadow circled the ship, hunting for its prey. Suddenly, razor-sharp teeth broke through the surface, gnashing at the air.

Hook yelped and cowered back. "No . . . please . . . don't let him get me!"

The fierce pirate captain—the one who had been terrorizing Barrie ever since that fateful trip to the museum—now looked like nothing more than a scared little kid.

"Wait, you're afraid of it, aren't you?" Barrie said. "Whatever is down there?"

Barrie stood up, feeling how unsteady his legs were. They were shaking from adrenaline and fear, a potent combination. But he also felt a strength in them that he didn't know he had. He clutched the hook in his hands. Rain pelted his face, soaking his clothes and hair.

Tick-tock. Tick-tock.

"No, he got a taste of me!" Captain Hook screamed. "He wants the rest."

Barrie stared down at the pirate, who no longer seemed so terrifying. Everything suddenly made sense as all the pieces clicked into place in his head.

"Is that how you lost your hand?" Barrie asked, raising his voice to be heard over the storm.

"That's all he got," Hook cried out, brandishing his bloody stump. He clutched it closer to his chest, shivering from fear. "But he won't stop until he's got the rest."

Suddenly, Barrie realized something amazing—he'd just solved his first real mystery. And not just any mystery, but the mystery of Captain Hook and his missing hand. He was just like the kid detectives in his books. He'd solved a case that even real historians couldn't solve. He felt satisfaction course through him, but then a rush of fear snapped him out of it.

Barrie fixed his eyes on Captain Hook, who continued to grovel in the shadows, cowering back from the water. Hook was afraid of the ticking and the water, but as soon as that creature left, the pirate captain would recover— and he'd probably be even angrier than before.

Barrie felt afraid, but solving that mystery had given him a boost of courage. He fixed his eyes on the dark water. He knew that he had only one choice—and one way out.

He stepped onto the plank.

It wobbled under his feet. Below him, the waves frothed and churned angrily. The dark creature continued to circle.

Tick-tock. Tick-tock.

Barrie took a deep breath, inching out to the end of the plank. He waited for the next pass—*tick-tock*—then he tossed the rusty old hook into the water to distract it.

The creature thrashed in the waves, darting after the hook.

"Noooooooo—" Captain Hook screamed.

Barrie dove into the ocean, feeling the sharp sting of cold water envelop him. Right then, a huge wave slammed into him. The riptide caught his body, sucking him downward. He felt himself sinking further and further. He struggled to breathe but choked on more briny water.

White stars danced in front of his vision. He started to lose consciousness. His lungs were running out of oxygen.

This is it, he thought. *I'm going to drown.*

18

SECOND STAR TO THE FRIGHT

Barrie sank deeper into the black water. It choked him and clogged up his throat.

Panic gripped his heart and squeezed it tight. His body went rigid with fear. The water was opaque, almost black. Anything could be lurking down there—including that shadowy creature with the razor-sharp teeth. The hook had distracted it . . .

But for how long?

He gulped for oxygen, but only swallowed more salt water. It filled his lungs, bloating them. He couldn't tell which way was up. He thrashed around helplessly and started to black out, but then lightning pulsed overhead and helped to orient him.

He swam toward the light, fighting against the churning water, pumping his arms and struggling toward the surface. He swam harder and kicked his feet, propelling himself upward.

Right when his lungs were burning and starting to convulse, he burst through the surface and gulped down air, which tasted sweeter than any candy. He flailed around until he spotted the lights along the shoreline, and then he swam for it.

Waves slapped at his face. He sputtered but had no choice but to keep swimming. The only other option was to drown.

* * *

He glanced back. Behind him, the *Jolly Roger* continued to sail away, off toward that strange place from the map.

The place where you never grow up.

The ship bobbed and crested the waves, cutting through them like they were butter. Candlelight flickered in the captain's cabin. He could see Captain Hook's silhouette framed in the window.

Barrie felt a jolt of fear and dragged his gaze away.

He'd escaped from the ship just in time. Now he could grow up and join his friends in junior high in the fall, and eventually in high school, like Rita. He didn't care if it involved algebra and SAT prep classes, as long as he got to keep his friends. That was all that mattered.

He'd do a *million* math problems to keep Michael and John in his life.

That thought kept Barrie going, even as his arms burned from swimming and fighting against the waves. He finally reached the shore, climbing out and dragging himself onto the rocky beach.

His legs wobbled as he stepped onto the pebbles. It felt like he was still out at sea, rocking on the pirate ship, even though he was standing on dry land.

He climbed up the embankment and clambered onto the sidewalk, dripping a trail of water behind him. The marina was mostly deserted now. It was late. A thin sliver of moon hung in the dark sky.

He expected Michael and John to burst out of hiding and greet him. Now that he was safe, he was excited to recount his adventures battling Captain Hook. It was like one of their video games, except this was real.

He looked for Rita's car, which should be idling by the side of the road. She'd be annoyed that he was late, but mostly relieved that he was okay. Not because she cared about him—but because their parents would definitely ground her if she lost her brother at the marina.

The last thing she wanted was to get grounded and not be able to smooch Todd.

But there were no signs of Michael and John, or Rita and her car, which was easy to spot due to its bright blue paint. In fact, the whole marina was eerily deserted. Streetlamps shone down, creating pools of light. The streets were empty. The shops were all closed.

How long was I on that ship?

Barrie racked his brain. He couldn't be sure, but it wasn't more than two hours. Right?

"Michael! John!" Barrie called, searching the marina. "I made it—our plan worked. You can come out now!"

But still nothing.

Where did they go?

He scanned the area again for any sign of his friends. Then he tried again. "Hey, I'm right here. You can come out now—"

Suddenly, a dark shadow fell over him.

"Kid, what're you doing out here?"

Barrie whipped around, expecting Captain Hook. But his eyes fell on—

A security guard.

He breathed a sigh of relief. This was a different guard from the one who had been patrolling the marina earlier. He was tall and skinny with a bushy mustache and a Pirates baseball cap.

"Hey, kid, the museum's closed," the guard said, glowering at him. "You can't be out here. Especially in this storm."

Overhead, the sky crackled and rumbled with lightning and thunder.

"Sir, I'm lost . . . and my ride isn't here for some reason," Barrie said. "I need you to help me get home."

The guard looked suspicious for a moment, but then he softened. "Okay, kiddo. What's your parents' number?"

Barrie recited their numbers by heart and waited while the guard tried them.

I was probably just on the ship longer than I realized, he thought. He had lost consciousness, after all. Most likely,

Rita had taken Michael and John home before they missed their curfew. She'd come back and get him. But Barrie was freezing and soaking wet. He didn't want to wait for her. He wanted to go home now. Nothing sounded better right now than his own bed.

The guard waited while the phone rang. Then, he lowered it from his ear.

"Kid, there's no answer at these numbers," the guard said, disconnecting the second call. "Look, I'm not falling for this prank again—"

"Sir . . . it's not a prank," Barrie stammered. "I swear I'm really lost. The storm probably messed up the phones. Look, please gimme a ride home."

The sky was still thick with clouds. Lightning pulsed, illuminating the bay at random intervals, while thunder rocked the ground. Wisps of rain pelted the marina, whipped up by the wind.

The guard narrowed his eyes. For a second, Barrie thought he was going to tell him to get lost. But then he softened.

"Fine, let's go," he said, leading Barrie to the parking

lot. They piled into his patrol car, which wasn't very impressive.

Barrie watched as the lights of the bay faded out of sight, as the car wound through their quaint town heading for his home. But before they vanished, he could've sworn that in a flash of lightning, he spotted the *Jolly Roger* bobbing in the distance, heading for the open ocean.

But in the blink of an eye, the ship was gone, as if it had vanished from this world altogether.

* * *

A few minutes and several turns later, the guard pulled into the cul-de-sac and around to the front of Barrie's house. The porch light was on, welcoming him home.

"Is this it?" the guard asked, tipping his hat toward the front door.

"Yes, sir," Barrie said, reaching for the door handle. "Thanks for the ride."

"Don't mention it," the guard said with a stiff nod. "Just be more careful, especially when there's a storm brewing. Anything could've happened to you. The marina can be a dangerous place for lost boys. We had a kid go missing some years ago. Terrible tragedy."

You have no idea, Barrie thought, remembering Captain Hook and the strange creature in the water. But he knew better than to mention any of that. Nobody would ever believe him.

Except for Michael and John, of course. That's why they were best friends.

"I will. I promise," Barrie said instead. And he meant it.

He'd had more than enough adventures for one day. No, scratch that.

For one *lifetime.*

As he climbed from the patrol car and watched it speed away, Barrie had never felt so glad to be home. Every muscle in his body screamed in pain from his swim through the bay and his narrow escape from Captain Hook. His clothes were still sopping wet and growing stiff from salt.

I'll even be happy to see Rita, he thought with an incredulous smile as he headed for the front door. And he'd never—like never ever not even once—felt happy to see his sister before.

But her sky-blue car wasn't parked in the driveway.

Strange, he thought with a frown. She always parked there, while his parents used the two-car garage. But maybe she'd ended up going out with her friends. After all, she did have a later curfew now that she was sixteen. That could also be why she had forgotten to pick him up. Todd probably distracted her.

Ugh, gross.

Barrie reached the front door and fished his keys out of his pocket. He slid the key into the lock, but it didn't fit. It wouldn't even slide into the slot.

What the heck? He retracted it from the lock and examined it.

It looked normal enough, but maybe it had gotten damaged in the escape?

He rang the doorbell and knocked a few times, then waited. A few seconds later, he heard footsteps padding up to the door. Then the deadbolt twisted.

The door cracked open.

Warm light spilled out onto the porch. Barrie was momentarily blinded. But then, when his vision cleared, what he saw shocked him.

An older woman's face peered out of the crack in the doorway.

"Uh, can I help you?" she asked, sounding worried. "What's a nice young man like you doing out so late?"

"Right . . . I live here," Barrie said, backing away. "This is my house."

He scanned the address, but he was sure this was the right place. He knew his own house. He'd lived there his whole life.

"What do you mean?" the old woman said, adjusting her glasses. "I think you've made a mistake. Young man, are you feeling okay?"

"Wh-where are my parents?" Barrie stammered, feeling alarmed. "Where's my sister? What did you do with them?"

"*Do* with them?" she asked with a frown. "Why, whatever do you mean?"

"The *Darlings*," Barrie said, plowing ahead. "This is our house! Where are they?"

"Oh, that name does ring a bell," she said with a curt nod. "We bought the house from them. But that was ages ago—"

"No . . . that's impossible," Barrie said. "I was here earlier today! My family lives here. This is our house!"

"Well, there must be some mistake," she said, pursing her lips. "The Darlings haven't lived here in a very long time."

"Wait . . . what do you mean?" Barrie said, his mind reeling and struggling to process what she was saying.

"I believe they moved into the retirement community across town," she went on. "The nice one across from the park. I heard their daughter married a local fellow and lives in another state with her husband and kids. Let me see what was his name? Oh, Ted . . . or Todd . . . something like that. You know how these real estate agents *love* to gossip—"

"*Retirement* community?" Barrie said, realizing what this meant—his parents had grown old. "Rita? Married? Kids?"

The horror of that struck him like a dagger to the heart.

"Come to think of it, there was this local tragedy a while back," the woman continued with a sad shake of her head. "Read about it in the papers long before we bought the house from them. They had a son. He was about your age, I reckon."

"A son?" Barrie choked out. Tears pricked his eyes.

"Yeah, he went missing down at the marina during a bad storm," she said. "But that was a few decades ago."

"He went missing?" Barrie repeated, his brain reeling from the information. Suddenly, he remembered what the security guard had said about the marina being dangerous for lost boys.

"Yup, he surely did," the woman said. "His name was . . . Barrie. Yes, that's it. Barrie . . . Darling. It was an awfully long time ago. But you don't forget something like that. Terrible tragedy, that was."

"They never found him?" Barrie said, the words coming out in barely a whisper.

She shook her head. "Nope, they never did find him. Not even a body. They think he must've fallen into the ocean and drowned. Awful, just an awful tragedy."

"No . . . he's alive," Barrie gasped. The words were

almost inaudible. "He didn't die . . . he just got a little lost . . . but he came home . . ."

"What was that, son?" the woman said, squinting at him suspiciously. She opened the door more to see him better. "Wait, what did you say your name was again?"

But Barrie could barely hear what she was saying. His ears were ringing from shock, drowning out her voice. Before she could interrogate him further, he bolted off down the street, heading for Michael's house, even though he feared what he would find there.

He cut through to the backyard and peered through the bedroom window, but there was no video game console or outer space comforter or skateboard lying by the door.

Instead, the bedroom was decorated with every shade of pink imaginable. A little girl with blond curls lay in the bed in a pale blue nightgown. Her father was perched on the edge, tucking her in. He had a receding hairline and wore glasses, but his face looked vaguely familiar.

"Daddy, tell me the one about Captain Hook and the Lost Boys again," she said, her curls bouncing angelically around her face. "That one's my favorite."

The father looked sad. "Once upon a time, my best friend Barrie found a rusty old pirate hook on a ship and made a wish to never grow up . . ."

Michael? Barrie stared at the middle-aged man in shock. That was his best friend?

Unable to believe his eyes, Barrie backed away from the window. The horror of it rushed through him. He looked down at his still child-sized hands. Even though it felt like he was only gone for a short time, decades had passed.

Michael had grown up and had a family of his own now, while Barrie hadn't aged a day. His parents were elderly and lived in a retirement community, while his sister was married with kids. In fact, everyone in his life had grown up, all while he was held captive on Captain Hook's ship. His wish to never grow truly had been a terrible curse. This was Hook's final revenge.

many incarnations, and whom I now get to bring to life in a brand-new context—and in our world. This is also the first Disney Chills book where I created an original pitch from scratch. It's been fun to see this series evolve.

Oh, and I always wanted to write a pirate book! Guess I can check that off my bucket list. Full disclosure: I thought they'd be space pirates—but Captain Hook is pretty darn cool.

I also want to thank my one-eyed pup, whom I often refer to as my pirate dog. He was at my feet for most of the drafting of this book, keeping me going on a tight deadline.

Dear readers, you made it this far in the series! Thank you for your continued support in picking up these scary, whimsical, creepy little books. We've got more villains coming for you!

Can't wait for you to find out what's next for Disney Chills.

Argh, matey!

ACKNOWLEDGMENTS

Everything starts with Disney Books—my amazing editor, Kieran Viola; my design team, who create the best covers ever; and my publicity team, who are working hard to get these books to readers, especially in a crazy time. I'm looking forward to working on more villains with you. Also, as always, thanks to my fantastic book agent, Deborah Schneider, and the rest of my team. Disney Chills takes a team, and I am thankful that I have such an incredible one behind me.

Writing Captain Hook was special for me, for many reasons. I'd be remiss if I didn't thank J. M. Barrie for creating these incredibly complex and iconic characters, who enriched my childhood and kept me entertained through